Carnival of Crime

Joe jumped out of the bumper car and began to hurry across the floor. This time he wasn't going to lose Farkas, the man he'd been following all day.

Frank was so startled to see Joe running in front of him that he spun his steering wheel and rammed into the wall. Moments later, a kid rammed his bumper car into Frank's car.

Joe was nearing the outer edge of the floor when some sixth sense warned him of danger. He looked back over his shoulder.

Joe realized that a driver in a baseball cap and sunglasses was steering his bumper car straight at him. And there was no room to dodge. In another moment, Joe would be crushed between the on-rushing car and the wall behind him.

The Hardy Boys Mystery Stories

Available from MINSTREL Books

THE HARDY BOYS® MYSTERY STORIES

122

The

HARDY
BOYS®

CARNIVAL OF
CRIME

FRANKLIN W. DIXON

A MINSTREL® BOOK

PUBLISHED BY POCKET BOOKS

New York   London   Toronto   Sydney   Tokyo   Singapore

This book is a work of fiction. Names, characters, places, and incidents are either the product of the author's imagination or are used fictitiously. Any resemblance to actual events or locales or persons, living or dead, is entirely coincidental.

A MINSTREL PAPERBACK *ORIGINAL*

A Minstrel Book published by
POCKET BOOKS, a division of Simon & Schuster Inc.
1230 Avenue of the Americas, New York, NY 10020

Copyright © 1993 by Simon & Schuster Inc.

Front cover illustration by Daniel Horne

Produced by Mega-Books of New York, Inc.

ISBN: 0-671-79312-8

First Minstrel Books printing October 1993

10 9 8 7 6 5 4 3 2 1

THE HARDY BOYS MYSTERY STORIES is a trademark of Simon & Schuster Inc.

THE HARDY BOYS, A MINSTREL BOOK, and colophon are registered trademarks of Simon & Schuster Inc.

Printed in the U.S.A.

Contents

CARNIVAL OF
CRIME

1 Fair or Foul?

Joe Hardy pulled the van into a vacant slot and said, "Here we are, guys. Opening night at the Bayport Fair, with the most death-defying rides of any traveling show in the nation."

"How do you know?" his older brother, Frank, demanded.

"The commercial on the radio said so," Joe shot back.

"There's a sucker born every minute," Frank teased, his brown eyes twinkling. "Since when did you start believing everything you hear on commercials, Joe?"

"I don't," Joe retorted. "That's why I wanted to come tonight—so I could test the rides myself and make sure they're as death-defying as they said."

From the backseat, the Hardys' friend Chet Morton

1

said, "I'll be testing the food stands. There's got to be a place that serves real Italian heroes, the ones with two kinds of ham, Genoa salami, provolone, mozzarella, peppers, onions, olive oil, vinegar . . ."

Joe groaned. "If there is, don't tell me about it," he pleaded.

The Hardys and Chet hopped out of the van and took a look at the brightly lit fairground. Joe read the huge banner above the entrance gate: "'Major Bowman's Fairs to Go.'"

"Bowman?" Frank repeated. "I know that name from somewhere."

Chet said, "Sure, everybody does. Major Bowman the Showman. He's famous—one of the last of the old-time carnival owners."

Frank said, "That's not why I know the name. Somebody named Bowman left a message on our answering machine this morning. Her name was Susan Bowman. I wonder if she's related," he added as they got on the ticket line.

They bought their tickets and joined a large crowd of spectators just inside the front gate. On a raised platform a six-piece brass band in gold-spangled uniforms was playing a catchy tune with lots of oompahs. Just in front of the band were four clowns on tall stilts, dancing to the music as they tossed rings, balls, and clubs back and forth among themselves.

"Hey, Joe," Frank said, pointing at a clown with hair that stuck up in green and purple spikes, "why don't you ask him where he got his hair done? Might make you more attractive to the girls."

2

Seventeen-year-old Joe glared at his brother, then ran his fingers through his blond hair and turned back to look at the clown. A length of chain served as a belt for the clown's black leather pants, and his matching vest was held closed by a gigantic safety pin. As the band played a rollicking tune, the clown kicked one stilted leg high in the air and spun completely around on his other stilt. He thrust both arms in the air, just in time to catch a tossed ring on each of them.

"How did he do that?" Joe said, his blue eyes wide with amazement.

"Practice," Chet replied. "Lots and *lots* of practice."

Just then the band finished and a pretty blond girl stepped onto the platform, facing the crowd. She was wearing a black top hat and a bright red coat trimmed with gold braid.

"Hey, everybody, welcome to the spectacular opening night of the annual Bayport Fair," she said into her microphone. "Are we going to have fun tonight?"

"Yes!" the audience shouted back.

"I can't hear you," she said, her blue eyes twinkling. "Are we going to have fun?"

"Yes!" the crowd roared back.

"That's better. This year's fair is brought to you by Major Bowman's Fairs to Go, the most famous traveling show in the world. And you've just been watching the most famous clown family in the world, the Four Fratelli Brothers. Let's hear it for the Fratellis!"

Joe, Frank, and Chet joined the cheers and ap-

3

plause. The four stilt-walking clowns bowed so low that Joe couldn't understand why they didn't fall on their faces. Then one of the clowns, who was in whiteface, snatched the blond girl's top hat and tossed it in the direction of the one dressed in black leather, who caught it on his spiked hairdo. He in turn sailed it back toward the girl. She grinned and caught it one-handed, flipped it up in the air, and it landed on her head. There were more cheers and laughter from the crowd.

"All right, people," the girl continued. "Enough clowning around. I know you're all dying to check out some of the most challenging games of skill and most thrilling, death-defying rides you'll find anywhere on earth."

"She must have written that commercial you heard," Chet whispered to Joe.

"Remember, we also offer an amazing variety of delicious snacks to fit every appetite," she added.

"She wrote that part especially for you," Joe whispered back.

"And don't forget, folks—at ten o'clock sharp, Major Bowman's Fairs to Go brings you a fabulous fireworks spectacular that you'll be talking about for years." There was a drum roll. The blond girl raised her voice and added, "It's all here, and it's all for you, at the one and only Bayport Fair!"

The cymbals crashed and the trumpets blared, then the band struck up a fast tune. The girl stepped back, and the four clowns began to do a chorus-line kick routine. Still on stilts, the four turned slowly in a

4

circle, ending up where they had started. Then they, the band, and the girl marched off down the midway. Most of the crowd followed.

"I wonder who that girl was?" Chet said, as the music faded. "She looks about our age. How'd she get to be head of the show?"

"Whoever she is, I wonder if she's had the job long," Frank mused. "Did you notice that her coat was about five sizes too big? I'll bet it was made for somebody else."

"Don't you guys ever stop detecting?" Chet kidded. Chet knew that if he hung out with the Hardys, sooner or later they would encounter a case to investigate. Frank and Joe had picked up their detective skills from their father, a former New York City cop who'd become a private investigator.

"Come on, let's have some fun," Chet said.

As they walked, Joe surveyed the fairground, which was laid out like a little town. Most of the rides, games, and food concessions fronted on one of the three main avenues, labeled West Avenue, East Avenue, and, down the center, the Midway. Numbered cross streets, lined with smaller booths, linked the wide avenues.

As the three turned onto one of the side streets, Joe heard someone shout, "Hey, boys, don't pass by without checking me out!" Joe glanced over his shoulder and saw a tall, thin man in a loud plaid suit behind the counter of a shooting gallery.

"Come on over, guys," the carny said into a mega-phone. "Here's your big chance to test your skill and

5

win valuable prizes for all your girlfriends. Who's going to be the first?"

He picked up one of the air rifles on the counter and offered it to Frank, who was closest to the booth. "Here you are, my friend," he continued. "Five tries for two dollars, less than fifty cents a try. Three hits gets you your choice of a valuable prize. Four hits and you win a large bear."

"Sure, why not?" Frank said. He pulled two bills from his pocket and took the rifle from the barker.

Joe looked inside the booth and saw the usual revolving targets and lines of moving duck figures. Above them, on a high shelf, were four plush bears the size of full-grown Saint Bernard dogs. One was bubble gum pink, one was Day-Glo orange, and the other two were lime green with purple bellies.

The carny reached down behind the counter and took out five plastic pellets, which he loaded into the air gun. "There you are, my friend," he said to Frank. "Show your buddies what real shooting looks like."

Frank took careful aim and pulled the trigger. One of the moving ducks promptly fell over.

"Way to go," Chet exclaimed, just as Frank fired again and knocked over another duck.

"I can see I've got an expert here," the man said loudly, attracting the attention of other fair-goers. "Come on over, folks, and watch the sharpshooter at work. One more hit, he wins a valuable prize. *Two* more hits, and he gets to take home a large bear."

Frank's next shot also knocked over a duck.

6

"There you go, you are definitely a prizewinner!" the man exclaimed. "One more hit wins the large bear."

"Come on, Frank," Joe teased. "Just think how great it would be to have that orange bear with you when you go to sleep at night."

"I'll deal with you later," Frank muttered. He raised the air gun again. By now a small crowd had gathered to watch.

Frank fired, but the duck sailed on untouched. Somebody in the little crowd muttered, "Aw, tough."

"Don't let it bother you, my friend," the man said. "You still have another chance at the large bear, and remember, you're already a guaranteed prizewinner. Take your time, take your time."

Frank aimed his last shot and squeezed the trigger. The duck, still upright, glided out of sight.

The man in the booth reached for Frank's rifle and said, "Hard luck, my friend. Your three hits entitle you to any of these wonderful souvenirs of the fair." He pointed to a shelf full of small, tacky-looking plastic dolls and animals.

"But . . ." the carny continued, "since this is opening night, I'll tell you what I'm going to do. If you want to try again, I'll count two of your three hits toward the bear. Just make two more hits out of five, and the large bear is yours!"

"Go ahead, Frank," Chet urged, putting two dollars on the counter. "My treat."

The man in the booth took out another five pellets

and put them in the rifle, then handed it back to Frank. On his first shot, one of the ducks fell over. But none of the other four shots connected.

"Hard luck, sport," the man said. "But I'll tell you what, I'll make the same deal with you again. Two hits still count toward the bear. Just two more, and it's yours. What do you say?"

Grim-faced, Frank put two more dollars on the counter. Once again, only one of his five shots knocked over a duck. "That's it for me," he announced.

"How about your friends?" the man asked, taking the rifle from Frank. "One of you boys like to test your skill and win a large bear?"

Joe stepped forward. "I'll give it a try," he said, taking the air gun. The man reached under the counter for five more pellets. As he was about to put them in the rifle, Joe stuck out his hand and said, "Can I have a look at those?"

"Sorry, friend," the man said quickly, taking a step backward. "I'm the only one who's allowed to load the rifles. It's a basic safety rule."

"What's wrong, Joe?" Chet demanded.

"A couple of those pellets have nicks in them," Joe said in a loud voice. "They're damaged, probably deliberately. That's why he won't let me see them. An Olympic medalist wouldn't hit a target with one of those pellets."

"Now hold on, buddy," the man said in an ugly voice. "Just because your friend couldn't hit the broad side of a barn, that doesn't give you the right to make accusations against me."

"That's the funny part," Frank said, standing shoulder to shoulder with Joe. "On my last round, I deliberately aimed to miss. And one of those ducks fell over anyway. What is it—a button on the floor that knocks them over when you press it?"

"You mean the game is fixed?" Chet cried out.

"From start to finish," Frank replied, turning to the crowd. "What this guy does is let the shooter get three hits, then sucker him into buying more rounds by keeping him just short of enough hits to win a bear."

"You're calling my show rigged?" the man growled.

"Yeah, that's right," Joe answered. "Everybody comes close, but nobody ever wins. Those bears must have about five years worth of dust on them."

"Okay, wise guys," the man hissed. "You asked for it." He reached under the counter and produced a baseball bat. "Get away from my stand, or I play hardball with your heads!"

2 Wheel of Danger

Joe risked a quick glance over his shoulder. A small group of people were gathered in a semicircle, waiting to see what would happen.

Frank tensed, ready for the guy to take a swing. "This man is threatening us," he called to the crowd. "And you're all witnesses. He's trying to stop us from telling people that his shooting gallery is rigged."

The carny reddened. "These guys are just a bunch of troublemakers," he said loudly. "This is an honest test of skill. I challenge any of you to try it— absolutely free."

At that a teenage boy with long black hair and a heavy-metal T-shirt stepped forward. "Let me have a try," he mumbled.

The carny handed him the air gun. The boy fired off five rapid shots. Each one knocked over a duck.

"A fantastic performance, my friend," the man in the plaid suit said, shooting Joe and Frank a look full of hostility. Then he asked the long-haired boy, "Which of these wonderful large bears would you like for your prize?"

A few moments later, the boy was walking off with a green and purple stuffed bear under his arm.

"All right, friends," the man called, deliberately ignoring Joe and Frank. "Who's next?"

"Come on," Frank muttered to Joe and Chet. "Let's get out of here."

As they walked away, Chet said, "I thought you said the game was fixed. That guy won, didn't he?"

Joe gave a snort. "He sure did," he said. "But don't be surprised if that bear he carried off is back on the shelf by tomorrow night."

Chet looked confused.

"What Joe's saying is that that guy was probably a shill," Frank explained. "He's a decoy planted in the crowd, and he works with the guy running the booth. The kid won to make it look as though the game was honest and that we were just a couple of sore losers."

"That's rotten," Chet said. "Are all the games here rigged?"

"Doubtful," Frank replied. "I imagine most of the carnies are honest. But that doesn't mean you won't find a couple of rotten apples." He added, "Let's remember to report this before we leave tonight, okay?"

Chet made a face. "I think I need something to take

my mind off that nasty guy. Why don't we go down that way?"

Joe looked in the direction Chet was pointing and laughed. Fifty feet away, smoke was rising from a shish kebab stand.

"Get serious," Joe teased. "We had burgers just before we came here."

"That was at least an hour ago," Chet protested, moving toward the stand. Joe caught Frank's eye and shrugged. They followed their friend over and waited while he ordered a shish kebab on pita bread with grilled onions and sesame sauce, then the three of them continued to explore the fair.

Chet finished his snack and tossed the paper in a litter basket. "Let's check out the Ferris wheel," he suggested.

Joe glanced down the midway to where the big wheel—its shape outlined in multicolored lights— slowly revolved. As he watched, it came to a stop. "That's a ride for kids," he said to Chet. "Let's go on a serious ride like the Zipper."

"Give me a break," Chet protested. "I just ate a shish kebab."

Joe reluctantly agreed, and they headed for the ride.

At the Ferris wheel, they bought tickets and joined the line. Just ahead of them, a boy of about eight was standing next to a teenage girl. Joe heard him say, "Are you sure you won't come with me, Kate?"

"No way, Billy," she replied. "Heights make me sick to my stomach."

Billy grinned and said, "Not me, Sis. The higher the better."

"That's the spirit," Joe said, grinning down at the boy.

As each of the gondolas reached the ground, the Ferris wheel stopped to let passengers get off and others get on. A cheerful-looking woman in a red jumpsuit was collecting tickets. Every time she turned her head, her big gold hoop earrings—three in each earlobe—jingled and her dark ponytail bounced on her shoulder.

When she got to the two kids in front of Joe, the girl handed her one ticket and her little brother started to climb in. The woman looked surprised, but she helped him into his seat and pulled the safety bar down across his waist.

"There you are," the woman said. "Have fun."

"Bye!" the boy called to his sister as the wheel began to turn. "Wave to me when I'm way up there!"

The woman in the jumpsuit turned to Joe, Frank, and Chet. "These gondolas only seat two," she said, with a smile that revealed white, even teeth. "Who wants to go up alone?"

Joe glanced over at Frank, then said, "I'll volunteer." He climbed in and latched the safety bar himself.

The wheel turned, then paused, leaving Joe at the level of the fairground roofs. He glanced down and exchanged grins with Frank and Chet, who were just climbing into the next gondola.

As soon as all the gondolas were filled, the giant

13

wheel began to revolve at a steady pace. At the top of the arc, the lights of Bayport and the surrounding towns seemed to go on forever. Joe wondered if he should come back for another ride in daylight. He was curious to find out if he could see his house.

Joe was just beginning to pick out a few landmarks when his gondola started down again, into the glare and bustle of the midway. The sounds of laughter from the bumper cars and squeals of fright from the Fighter Jet ride grew louder, along with the calliope music from the merry-go-round and the distant oompah of the brass band. Joe took a deep breath. The air smelled of popcorn and hot dogs.

As Joe's gondola neared the top for the third time, he noticed Billy, the little boy in the gondola just ahead of his, leaning over the side to wave to his sister on the ground. Joe was about to tell him to be careful when he heard a loud sound like the grinding of gears. The wheel gave a sickening lurch and stopped. Some of the passengers cried out in alarm.

"Keep cool, people," came a shout from the ground. Joe craned his neck to look. It was the woman in the red jumpsuit.

"We've got a minor problem here, nothing to worry about," she continued. "The wheel will be moving again in a minute."

A minute passed, then another. Joe noticed that Billy, apparently bored by the delay, was starting to rock his gondola back and forth. Joe smiled. He and Frank used to do that, too, when they were Billy's age.

14

They'd wait to see which of them would chicken out first.

Joe glanced over his shoulder and called out to Frank and Chet, whose gondola was a few feet lower than his. "Hey, guys, don't you wish we'd brought along a couple of hang gliders?"

"Not me," Chet called back. "I'll leave that daredevil stuff to you. I'm just sorry I didn't bring a hot dog up."

Suddenly Frank yelled, "Joe! That kid in the next car—something's wrong!"

Joe turned around.

Billy was leaning over the side of the gondola, his face deathly white. "Kate! Kate!" he shouted toward the ground. "Help, get me out of here! I feel dizzy. I think I'm going to be sick."

"Hey, Billy, take it easy," Joe called to the frightened boy. "You'll be okay. Just sit back and take a deep breath."

Billy looked back at him with wide eyes. "I'm scared, I want to go home," he said. "We're going to be stuck up here forever!" Tears started to flow down his cheeks.

"Impossible," Joe said. "I have to be home by ten." He wished he felt as lighthearted as he was trying to sound. This delay was really dragging out.

"Kate, help!" Billy shouted again, leaning even farther over the side of the gondola.

Just then, the boy's safety bar came unlatched. Joe gasped as the bar swung freely and banged against the

15

front of the gondola. Billy, who had been putting all his weight against the bar, was thrown forward. The front wall of the gondola kept him from falling, but his head and upper body were dangling over the edge. He let out a shrill wail.

"That kid! He's going to fall!" someone shouted from the ground. "Quick, somebody, do something! Help him!"

Joe's mind raced. Could he manage to convince Billy to sit down and refasten the safety bar? He was about to give it a try when he saw that the terrified child was struggling to his feet. His gondola started to rock back and forth wildly. Billy, eyes tightly shut, swayed with it. One wrong move, and—

Joe hastily sized up the situation. The boy's gondola was only about eight feet in front of his, and slightly lower. Could he manage to cross the gap? If he stood on the seat, he could reach one of the two rims of the wheel and swing himself along, hand over hand. Halfway between the two gondolas was one of the girders that served as spokes to the wheel. If he needed to, he could wrap his legs around it for support.

As quickly as he thought of the plan, he put it into motion. He hit the release of his safety bar and sprang up. Gripping the left-hand support rod, he climbed up onto the seat and reached for the steel rim of the wheel. He slid his right hand along the rim as far as he could, got a solid grip, and prepared to launch himself into space.

At that instant, the wheel gave a backward lurch

16

and Joe was thrown forward. He felt his feet graze the front rail of the gondola. Then his legs were swinging free, and he was dangling by his hands, fifty feet in the air. As the sound of screams reached him from the ground, he felt the rough steel of the rim biting into his hands. Then his fingers started to slip.

In another moment, he was going to fall!

3 The Carny's Warning

As Joe tightened his grip, he heard Frank call, "Hang on, Joe! I'm there already!"

Joe glanced over his shoulder. Frank was standing up in his gondola, reaching for the rim of the wheel. He was about to try the same maneuver that had just ended in disaster for Joe.

"No!" Joe shouted back. "I'll be all right." He wasn't at all sure about that, but he was glad to see Frank sitting back down in his gondola.

Blocking out the growing chorus of screams from the ground, Joe took a deep breath and tried to think clearly. His best hope was to get back to his own gondola and hope that Billy would have the sense to sit down and hold on.

Joe looked down. The gap between his feet and the front edge of the gondola was about two feet wide. He knew it wasn't much, but from his perspective, it looked like the Grand Canyon's little brother. What he had to do was swing in that direction, then let himself drop into the gondola. The thought of releasing his grip on the rim and letting himself fall made him swallow convulsively.

Time was running out; Joe's fingers were beginning to cramp. Taking a deep breath, he jackknifed at the hips, then let the weight of his legs start his body swinging back and forth. The pressure on his fingers grew almost unbearable. Just when he was sure that he could not stand it any longer, he sensed that his feet were over the gondola.

He released his grip on the rim, launched himself in the direction of the gondola, and for a moment was airborne. For one endless, terrifying moment, he was sure he had misjudged. Then his feet hit the floor of the gondola and the edge of the seat slammed into his knees. He grabbed the side of the gondola and let himself slump down onto the seat.

After a few seconds, he wiped the sweat out of his eyes and looked around.

Billy was kneeling on the seat of his own gondola, staring at Joe wide-eyed. "Wow!" he said. "That was really something! Are you okay?"

Joe gave a nod. "I'm fine," he called back. "How about you? Will you sit down and hold on until we get back down?"

The boy nodded. Just then, the Ferris wheel gave another lurch and started to revolve.

Joe watched as Billy's gondola reached the ground.

19

When Joe got to the landing stage, he saw the boy clutching his sister, while the woman in the red jumpsuit patted his shoulder.

"You nearly gave me a heart attack," the woman said to Joe, restarting the wheel to let Frank and Chet reach the landing.

Frank overheard. "Make that two heart attacks," he said as he climbed out of his seat.

"No, three," Chet insisted.

An angry-looking man with two small children in tow interrupted. "Hey," he said, waving three tickets for the Ferris wheel. "I want my money back. That thing's not safe!"

"The wheel is perfectly safe," the woman in red replied. "It's inspected regularly. But of course I'll refund your money."

The man took the money and stalked away. Frank asked, "Why did the ride stop and start like that? What was the problem?"

The woman frowned and said, "It was a minor glitch in the control box, that's all. Nothing to worry about. I've been running this wheel for ten years without any mechanical trouble."

"Do you mean you managed to fix it?" Joe asked.

"Sure," she said, but Frank noted that the expression on her face was anything but sure. "We've got mechanics and electricians on staff, but we don't bother them with minor problems."

"It looked pretty major to me," Chet said.

With a set face, the woman said, "The wheel

20

stopped for a couple of minutes, then started again. There wouldn't have been any problem at all if everyone had just relaxed and stayed put." She glared at Joe.

"Not quite," Joe replied. "That kid's safety bar came unlatched by itself. He was in real danger. That's why I did what I did."

Worry replaced anger on the woman's face. "I didn't know about that part," she admitted. "I couldn't see it from down here. That shouldn't have happened. I'll have to check all the latches tonight."

A blond girl in jeans and an orange Fairs to Go T-shirt hurried over to them. "Althea, what happened?" she demanded.

Joe realized that she was the same girl who had welcomed everybody to the fair earlier, only in different clothes.

"This guy here tried to rescue a little kid who got scared, and he nearly fell," Althea said. "It's okay, though. Nobody's hurt."

The girl turned to Joe and said, "I'm Susan Bowman, the manager of Fairs to Go. I'm sorry you had a bad experience just now. I hope you'll accept—"

Frank broke in. "Susan Bowman? You left a message on our machine this morning. I'm Frank Hardy, and this is my brother, Joe. And that's our friend Chet."

Susan's eyes grew wide, and then an expression of relief crossed her face. "Hey, am I glad to meet you! Do you have a couple of minutes to come to my office? I want to talk to you about something."

Frank met Joe's eyes, then said, "Sure, let's go."

Susan hesitated, glancing at Chet. "Er—" she began.

Chet spoke up. "I want to check out the taco stand. I'll meet you there when I'm done, okay?"

"Good idea," Susan said quickly. "Tell Paul, the guy behind the counter, to give you a taco on me."

"Thanks, I'll do that," Chet said, and walked away.

As the Hardys set off after Susan, Joe noticed a burly guy with a crew cut and a snake tattooed on his left forearm. He was leaning against the Ferris wheel ticket booth and scowling at the Hardys. As far as Joe knew, he'd never seen the guy before in his life. So why was he glaring at them with such hostility?

Just east of the last row of concessions was a parking lot full of trailers and campers. Susan led them to one of the trailers and opened the front door. The space inside was only big enough for a small desk, three folding chairs, and a file cabinet. The floor was covered with worn indoor-outdoor carpeting. She motioned for the Hardys to sit down, but she remained standing.

"I need help," Susan said. "A friend who lives around here told me you guys are terrific detectives. It looks more and more like that's what I need."

"What's the trouble?" Frank asked.

"Maybe nothing, but . . ." She paced over to the open window and stood with her back to them. "Four months ago, my dad, Major Bowman, had a heart attack. He's pulled through okay, but the doctors told him he needs to rest. That's why I took over running the show."

Joe thought she looked about eighteen. "You're pretty young for so much responsibility, aren't you?" he asked.

Susan spun around. Her cheeks were pink. "What's my age got to do with it?" she said angrily. "For your information, I've been working and hanging around Fairs to Go since I was old enough to walk. I know the show backward and forward, and I love it too much to let it go down the tubes. Especially now, when my dad isn't well. Does that answer your question?" she added, eyeing first Joe and then Frank.

"Hey, I didn't mean—" Joe began.

"It's okay," Susan said, rubbing her forehead. "It's just that everybody is saying that, and I'm sick of it. I *know* I can keep the show going, but somebody doesn't want me to. I need you to find out who and stop him, while there's still time. Will you help me? Please?"

Frank glanced over at Joe, who nodded. "We'll do what we can," Frank said. "But first we need to know what the problem is."

Susan leaned against the edge of her desk. "Maybe I'm making a big deal out of nothing, but more and more things are going wrong. Little things, mostly. Machinery that stops working, supply orders that get sent to the wrong place, minor accidents. So far, nothing major."

"Can you be more specific?" Frank asked.

23

"Oh, just one example," Susan said. "Two days ago was our last day at a town about fifty miles from here. First, somebody mixed up two bags, and we ended up with a couple hundred boxes of popcorn with sugar on it instead of salt. Then, the power went out at the Fighter Jet ride, stranding a couple of kids fifty feet up. And just when we got that fixed, the PA system went haywire, blasting everybody's eardrums."

"How long ago did these accidents start?" Joe asked.

"About a week after I took over the show," Susan replied. "I wonder about that. We carnies can be a superstitious bunch, you know. I've already heard whispers that FTG is jinxed, or that I am. And rumors are spreading to the public, too. Our gate receipts are starting to drop. If I don't stop this right now, everything could fall apart. The people who run the rides and the midway games are free agents. If our fair isn't drawing enough business, they might just leave us for another outfit. Without rides and stuff, our bookings will get worse. And if they get too bad, we'll have to fold. That would just about kill my dad."

"Do you think somebody is deliberately trying to wreck Fairs to Go?" Joe asked. "Who? And why?"

She gave a helpless shrug. "That's the problem! Who? I have no idea. We've got some competitors in the business who might like to see us in trouble, and I guess somebody here could be working for one of them, but—"

Just then, the office door opened. Joe turned around to see a middle-aged man with a fringe of

24

graying hair enter. The man glanced curiously at Frank and Joe, then said, "Oh, sorry, Susan. I didn't know you were busy. I wanted to go over our schedule with you."

"That's okay, Morris, we won't be long," Susan replied. "Frank, Joe, this is my dad's partner, Morris Tuttle. He handles the business side of the show. I don't know what we would do without him."

To Morris, she said, "I'm hoping Frank and Joe will find out who's trying to wreck Fairs to Go."

"You know, Susan, I'm not sure anybody is," Morris said. "I'm inclined to believe all these accidents are just—accidents. But I guess it can't do any harm to check out the possibility that someone's up to dirty tricks," he added.

Morris edged past Joe's chair and opened a door on the far side of the tiny room. Before the man closed the door, Joe caught a glimpse of another, even tinier office—just big enough for a desk, a chair, and a computer.

Frank coughed. "You know, Susan, if we're going to help you, it's probably better if you don't tell people about our investigation," he said in a low voice. "The bad guys are more likely to make a slip if they don't know we're after them."

"Oh, I'm sorry," Susan said, wide-eyed. "I didn't think. I was just so glad you agreed to help that I had to share the news with Morris. But I'll be more careful from now on, I prom—"

"Hold it," Joe interrupted. "I think we have an unwanted guest." He pointed to a shadow near the open window, then tiptoed over and leaned out. A guy in jeans and a plaid flannel shirt was just turning away. Joe reached out and grabbed his shoulder.

"Get your hands off me," the guy growled, spinning around and slapping at Joe's arm. He looked about twenty-three, with a pitted complexion, dark hair that needed a shampoo, and a scowling expression.

Susan hurried over. "Oh, it's you," she said in a tired voice. "Come in, Ricky. What can I do for you?"

"I want to know what this guy thinks he's doing, laying his hands on me like that," Ricky said, sticking his chin out. "Does he know who I am?"

"Sure I do. You're the guy I caught listening at the window," Joe retorted.

"This is Ricky Delgado," Susan explained. "He's my stepbrother."

"I'm part of the management of this show," Ricky announced. "Who are you guys, and what are you doing here?"

Instead of answering his question, Susan told Joe and Frank, "Ricky dropped out of business school to help me run the show after Dad got sick."

"Hey, get it straight. I took a leave of absence," Ricky corrected. "Listen, Susan, I need ten bucks, right away. Take it out of petty cash and put it against my salary."

Susan rolled her eyes, then took a ten-dollar bill from an envelope in her desk drawer and handed it to him.

"Thanks," he muttered, and slouched off after giving Joe another dirty look.

Joe continued to stand at the window and watch Ricky, to make sure that the guy didn't plan to hang around and eavesdrop some more. As Ricky was walking away, a tall, thin man in a gaudy plaid suit came up to him. Joe recognized him instantly as the man who ran the shooting gallery. The carny pulled out a sheet of paper and showed it to Ricky, jabbing it angrily with his forefinger. Then he looked over in the direction of the office trailer and recognized Joe at the window. With fists clenched and his face set in an angry glare, he hurried over to the trailer and flung the door open.

Susan sprang to her feet.

"What do you think you're doing, throwing me out of the show?" the man demanded loudly. "You'd better think again, or else you and all your little pals here are going to be very, very sorry!"

4 A Face in the Window

Bracing himself for action, Frank glanced quickly at Susan. Her face was pale, and she was breathing rapidly. But when she spoke, there was no hint of a tremor in her voice.

"You know the rules, Farkas," she said. "I don't allow any rigged games at Fairs to Go. I've watched you long enough to know that that shooting gallery you run is gaffed six ways to Sunday. A professional marksman couldn't win a prize unless you decided to let him."

"We noticed that, too," Frank said quietly. "We had a little run-in with this guy earlier this evening."

"That's a lie!" Farkas shouted, red-faced. "I run my operation the way I always have. The major never gave me any hassles, and I never gave him any. You've just got it in for me. That's why you're siding with these troublemakers."

"I don't know why my dad put up with you," Susan replied. "Maybe he didn't notice that your booth was crooked. Or maybe you played it a little straight when he was on hand. What happened, Farkas? Did you get greedier? Or did you figure you could put one over on me because I'm just a kid? Wrong. I'm carny born and bred, and I know as much as you do about gaffing a game. You've got two weeks to pack up and clear out, just the way that notice you're holding says."

Growling, Farkas crumpled up the paper and drew his arm back, as if to throw it at Susan. Frank quickly moved between the two of them. Joe joined him, shoulder to shoulder. The shooting gallery owner looked at the grim-faced six-footers and took a step backward.

"Tell your hired muscle here to butt out," Farkas said to Susan. "This is a private meeting between me and you."

"Meeting's over," Susan replied firmly. "Two weeks, Farkas. And if you make any more trouble, I'll have you thrown off the fairground immediately."

Farkas looked at her narrowly, then turned toward the door. "I'll remember this," he muttered, just before he slammed the door behind him.

Susan sighed and dropped into her chair. "I *hate* arguments."

"Well, I think you handled that like a pro," Joe said.

"Thanks," Susan said. "But I still wish it hadn't happened. Why can't people follow the rules?"

"You run an honest show, and that guy wants to make as much money as he can, honestly or not," Frank pointed out. "Farkas—is that his first or last name?"

"Hmm? Oh—last. His first name's Cecil, but everybody just calls him Farkas," Susan replied.

"Could he be behind the sabotage?" Frank asked. "He was really mad at you."

"I'll say," Susan said, with a sudden grin. Then the grin faded. "But I don't see why he'd want to wreck Fairs to Go. It was just this evening that I gave him the two weeks' notice. And as I said, these incidents started practically as soon as I took over the show. Up until tonight, Farkas had as much reason to want the show to be a success as anybody."

Frank nodded. "Good point—but we'll keep a close eye on him anyway. He sure doesn't wish you or the show well now."

Susan gave him a troubled look. "I hope you don't get the wrong impression about carnival folks," she said. "Farkas is an exception. Most of them are wonderful, friendly, honest people. But a cash operation like this that moves around a lot is bound to attract a few crooks. About the only thing we can do is keep an eye out for them, and weed them out when we spot them."

"Don't worry, we won't judge the others by him," Frank assured her. "And you can count on us."

"But we're going to need a lot more information,"

Joe said. "And I don't think we can just wander around asking people questions and expect to get anywhere. From what I've heard, carnival folks are pretty leery of outsiders."

"You got that right," Susan said. "Citizens, we call them. Let me think. . . . What if I say you're doing a class project on fairs? That way, you've got a legitimate reason to be here and to ask questions about how everything works."

"Sounds good," Frank said. "But will people buy it? Farkas has already seen us, and so did your brother and the woman at the Ferris wheel."

Susan grinned. "For all Farkas knows, you were here getting my permission to do your project when he barged in. And I don't care what Ricky thinks. As for Althea Coverdale, she heard me say I'd been trying to get in touch with you. If she asks, I'll just say it was to give you the go-ahead."

She pulled a pad out of her desk drawer. "I'll write out passes for you that will be good at all the attractions, and a note from me, asking people to help you with your project."

Joe accepted the papers. After exchanging goodbyes, Frank led the way out of the trailer. Outside, he turned to his brother and said, "The first thing we should do is find out more about why the Ferris wheel acted up."

"After that, we'd better retrieve Chet from the taco stand," Joe said. "I hate to think what might happen if we leave him there too long."

Althea was still at the controls of the Ferris wheel.

Joe showed her the note from Susan. After reading it through, she gave him and Frank a shrewd glance. "You're writing a term paper about fairs, are you?" she said. "I guess there are worse ways to spend your time."

"Did you track down the problem with the wheel?" Frank asked.

"I told you before," she replied. "There was a problem in the control box. I fixed it on the spot. After ten years, I know this wheel pretty well."

"What about the latch on the kid's safety bar?" Joe asked. "How did it fly open?"

"It was worn," she said shortly.

"Isn't the wheel inspected for worn parts?" Frank asked.

"You better believe it," she retorted. "I go over every gear, wire, and strut at least once every six months. But sometimes problems slip by. That must be what happened this time—unless somebody monkeyed with that latch."

"Why would anybody want to cause you that kind of trouble?" Frank asked.

"I don't know. I don't claim to get along with everybody in the world," Althea replied. "I never learned to put up with fools or crooks, and sometimes I'm a little too free about letting them see what I think of them. But I don't know anybody who'd want to ruin my operation and maybe get somebody badly hurt.

"Was there anything else?" she added. "I've got to get back to work."

"Thanks for your help," Frank said. "You really know your way around here, don't you?"

"I ought to," she replied. "I've been with the show ever since I was a kid. My first job was selling cotton candy, and I worked my way up to owning my own ride. Nobody's going to take away what I've earned, not without a real fight."

As the Hardys turned to go, Joe spotted the guy with the crew cut and snake tattoo again. He was leaning against a wire fence twenty feet away, watching them with a look of hatred on his face.

"What's the deal with that guy?" Joe asked Althea in an undertone.

She glanced over her shoulder, then turned back to the Hardys. "Oh, that's Raoul. Raoul Duchemin. He used to be a strongman in the show."

"Why does he look as if he wants to kill us?" Joe wanted to know.

Althea shifted uncomfortably. "Well . . . Raoul sort of has a crush on me. He doesn't like it when I talk to other guys."

Raoul pulled one of the metal fenceposts out of the ground. Still glaring at Joe and Frank, he held it in front of him, one hand on each end, and slowly bent it into the shape of a hairpin.

"*Used* to be a strongman?" Joe quoted.

Althea nodded, unaware of what Raoul was doing behind her back. "Uh-huh. He broke a couple of ribs one night during his act snapping chains around his chest. The doctors told him he'd damage himself for

33

good unless he quit doing his act. The carnival's the only life he knows, poor guy. He tried to turn himself into a clown, but he didn't have the knack. Now he just hangs around and helps out where he can."

Frank asked, "Is there any way Raoul could have monkeyed with the controls of the Ferris wheel?"

"Raoul?" Althea repeated. "I honestly don't think he'd be able to figure out how. In his strongman act, he used to break cement blocks with his forehead, if you catch my drift."

Now Raoul was straightening the fence post. Althea noticed Joe staring over her shoulder. "Raoul!" she exclaimed. "That's Fairs to Go property you just ruined. Shame on you!"

"Sorry, Althea," the ex-strongman muttered. "I didn't mean to." He looked down at the bent post, then dropped it on the ground.

"We'd better go," Frank said. "Our friend expected us to meet him about half an hour ago."

"Okay, enjoy yourselves," Althea said.

Chet was still waiting at the taco stand. His hands were empty. "Hey, where were you two?" he demanded. "Now that I took care of my appetite, I want to try a few rides."

For the rest of the evening, Joe kept a sharp lookout for any sign of trouble. He knew that Frank was doing the same. But nothing more happened to disturb the fun. Apparently, the troublemaker had gone off duty for the night.

* * *

When Frank and Joe got home after dropping Chet off, they found their mother in the living room looking through a magazine.

"How was the fair?" she asked.

"Part fun, part trouble," Joe said vaguely. "Where's Dad?"

"He's had a late meeting with some clients," Mrs. Hardy replied, then gave her sons a worried look. "You're not getting involved in a new case already, are you? You just finished that business of the mine fires over in Pennsylvania. Shouldn't you take a little time off?"

Frank was about to answer when there came a piercing shriek from the kitchen.

"It's Aunt Gertrude!" Joe exclaimed, already halfway out of the living room.

Inside the kitchen, Joe stopped so short that Frank, who was at his heels, rammed into him. Aunt Gertrude was by the table, clutching her face in her hands and staring wide-eyed at the window. Outside, there was a ghostly white face with exaggerated, brightly colored features. Its huge red lips were fixed in a demonic grin.

It was a clown, but a clown from a horror film.

With a loud, demented laugh, the clown turned and vanished into the darkness.

"What's going on?" Frank demanded.

"Let's find out!" Joe replied, racing toward the back door.

But once outside, they saw no sign of the sinister

35

clown. "Split up and circle the house," Joe shouted to Frank. "I'll take the driveway!"

"Right!" Frank replied, and ran off in the opposite direction.

As he rounded the corner of the house, Joe spotted the clown. It was halfway down the driveway, heading for the street. Joe put on an extra burst of speed. But just when he was even with the big elm tree and starting to gain on the intruder, his left foot caught on something. He let out a startled cry and tried to recover his balance, but couldn't. Desperately, he thrust his hands out in front of him to break his fall.

At that moment there was a blinding flash on Joe's right, followed a split second later by the roar of an explosion. Joe felt himself tossed into the air like a dead leaf in a windstorm.

5 Out of Control

Frank was on the other side of the house when he heard Joe's shout, followed closely by the noise of an explosion.

"Joe!" he yelled. He spun on one heel and ran full tilt in the direction of the sound. As he passed the kitchen door, his mother and aunt came rushing out onto the back porch.

"What is it? What happened?" Mrs. Hardy called to him. He had no time to answer. He raised his hand, signaling them to stay where they were, and ran on.

As Frank rounded the corner, he saw his brother sprawled on the concrete driveway at the foot of the old elm. He ran over to Joe, knelt down, and put his arm around his shoulders.

"Joe! Are you okay?" he demanded urgently.

Joe struggled to sit up. "Yeah, I think so," he said in a dazed voice. "What hit me?"

"I don't know, but I'm going to find out," Frank said grimly.

Joe shook his head. "That clown we saw—he must have set some kind of trap. And I fell right into it."

As if in response, the distant sound of mocking laughter reached them from the street. A second later, tires squealed as a car sped away.

"No point in chasing that clown on foot," Frank observed. "You didn't by any chance see who it was?" he added, hopefully.

"It could have been anyone under that clown makeup," Joe replied. "For what it's worth, though, the costume didn't look like any of the Fratellis'. But I guess they could have more than one outfit apiece."

Frank helped Joe to his feet. "Stay here," he said. "I'll turn on the floodlights."

But before he'd taken one step, the floodlights came on, illuminating the driveway. With the help of the lights, Frank could see that one side of the elm tree's trunk had been blackened, and a little patch of grass at its base had been burned away.

"Frank? Joe?" Mrs. Hardy called from the corner of the house. "Are you all right? Aunt Gertrude just called the police. They're on their way."

"We're fine, Mom," Frank called back.

"It was just somebody's idea of a joke," Joe added. "Don't worry about it."

"Yeah, some joke," Frank said softly. "Look at this, Joe."

Tied to the base of the tree was what was left of a large metal can. The force of the explosion had shattered it.

"And this must be what triggered it," Joe said, pointing to a thin length of nylon fishline that stretched across the driveway. One end was tied to a steel tent stake driven into the ground. The other was fastened to what was left of an electrical switch.

"Simple and clever," Frank said. "You tripped on the fishing line, that closed the switch, and the current set off the explosive. There must be a battery around here somewhere."

He started to circle the tree, then stopped. "Joe, look at this!" he exclaimed.

Joe rushed to his brother's side. Frank was pointing at a scrap of yellow paper that was pinned to the tree.

" 'Watch out, snoopers—we don't play FAIR. Get lost quick, or the next time won't be so funny,' " Joe read aloud.

"Block letters, in pencil," Frank observed. "Not much help there. It says *we* here. Must be more than one person involved. Is that printing on the other side?"

Joe craned his neck to look at the underside without touching the paper. "Yup. A leaflet advertising the Bayport Fair, by the looks of it."

"Maybe they weren't sure we'd catch their incredibly hilarious pun," Frank said dryly.

"We caught it all right," Joe growled. "And we're going to catch *them*, too."

A police car pulled up, its lights flashing, and two

officers got out. Frank was glad to see that one of them was Con Riley, who had given Frank and Joe his help on more than one of their cases.

The Hardys explained what had happened and showed the officers the note and the remains of the booby trap. Worried that police activity so early in the Hardys' investigation might muddy the waters, Frank suggested treating the incident as a practical joke.

"Pretty dangerous joke," Con Riley remarked. "But if no one files a complaint, it's none of our business. We'd better be moving."

"Do you mind if we keep the can and the note?" Joe asked.

"They're yours," Riley replied. "But watch your step, boys. I don't want to hear of any vigilante stuff. Catching criminals is police business."

After the two police officers left, Frank and Joe returned to the house, taking the note and the remains of the booby trap with them for later analysis. Aunt Gertrude was waiting in the kitchen with a plate of cookies and two glasses of milk.

"Here, boys," she said with a twinkle in her eye. "I always say that chocolate chips make you think more clearly." She added, "And now, if you'll excuse me, I'm going to bed. I've had about all the excitement I can stand."

Frank and Joe settled down at the kitchen table and started in on the cookies.

"Well," Joe began. "Our cover story lasted all of about thirty-six seconds. The question is, who saw through it?"

"There's Susan's partner, Morris Tuttle," Frank pointed out. "Remember? When he came into the office, she told him we were going to be looking into the sabotage."

Joe nodded. "Right. And let's not forget Susan's stepbrother, Ricky. I did catch him listening outside the window. He could have overheard the whole conversation. And he did seem like a creep."

"What about Farkas?" Frank asked. "He saw us in Susan's office, although I realize that's not enough to make him decide we're detectives. Still, he's mad at us in a big way for telling Susan about his rigged game."

"Ricky could have told him we were on the case," Joe pointed out. "I saw them talking together, after Ricky left the trailer. And what about Althea? Do you think she bought the story about our research project? If she didn't, she might have let something slip to that guy Raoul. And he's not exactly wild about us."

"Some cover," Frank grumbled. "Why didn't we just rent a billboard and announce that we were taking the case? It would have saved everybody a lot of trouble."

"True," Joe replied. "But look at it this way. Maybe we don't know enough yet to work up a solid list of suspects and motives, but we did find out one thing. After that clown's little attempt at humor, we can be sure that the stuff at the fair isn't just a string of unrelated accidents. Somebody really is trying to wreck Fairs to Go and doesn't want us to investigate."

"Right," Frank said. "And it's up to us to stop him,

before anyone gets hurt." He stood up and took his glass to the sink. "Let's turn in. Tomorrow we should hit the fairground bright and early."

At nine-thirty the next morning, Joe parked the van in a field near the front gate of the fairground. As he and Frank neared the entrance, a bearded man in jeans and a plaid flannel shirt blocked their path.

Oh, no, Frank thought, tensing up. Did we really have to start the day with a confrontation?

"Sorry, fellows," the bearded man said. "You'll have to come back in half an hour. The fair doesn't open until ten."

"That's okay," Frank said. "We're working here." He produced the passes Susan had written and introduced himself and Joe.

"Oh, sorry, Frank and Joe," the man said after looking over the passes. "Nobody told me. I'm Carl Orris. Nice to meet you. A research project, huh? What'll you be doing exactly?"

"Looking into how different parts of the show work and what different people do," Joe said. Grinning, he added, "I guess that means making pests of ourselves, asking a lot of questions."

Carl returned the grin. "I'll save you some trouble," he said. "Me, I'm head roustabout. When we move to a new town—which is every week or so—I look over the site and decide where all the rides and concessions should go. Then, after some major arguments with people who figure I should have given them a better spot—nearer the entrance or whatever—my crew and I help everyone set up."

"Have you been doing this a long time?" Frank asked.

"I've been with the show for about ten years," Carl replied. "But it was just last year that the major gave me this job. Before that, I was the original jack-of-all-trades. I sold hot dogs, emceed the freak show, repainted the horses on the merry-go-round . . . I even played the trombone in the band for a while. I was awful!"

Frank smiled, then said, "There've been a lot of accidents at Fairs to Go lately, haven't there?"

Carl's grin vanished instantly. "Where did you hear that?" he demanded.

"Around," Frank replied vaguely. "You know how it is. Is there any truth to the rumor?"

"I never pay attention to rumors," Carl said. "You guys shouldn't, either."

Frank pressed the point, saying, "A couple of people said they didn't think the accidents were really accidents. One guy even talked about a jinx."

Carl's face reddened, and the cords on his neck stood out. "Some people have mouths that are bigger than their brains," he retorted. "There is no—repeat, *no*—jinx on this show. And the next one who says there is, you tell them to say it to me . . . if they've got the guts to!"

"Yeah, we'll do that," Joe said, tugging at Frank's sleeve. "We'd better go. I bet you have a lot to do before the fair opens for the day."

As they walked into the fairground, Frank murmured, "Why did you drag me away like that? I had lots more questions to ask him."

"Me, too," Joe replied. "But not in the mood he's in. He's one of the only friendly people we've met here so far. Why get *him* mad at us, too?"

Frank was about to reply when someone bumped into him and stepped hard on his right foot.

"Hey, why don't you watch where you're going?" Frank demanded.

Ricky Delgado and two other guys were blocking the walkway. The guy who had stepped on Frank's foot was a little under six feet tall, with the shoulders and biceps of somebody who worked out. His blond hair was shaved very short on the sides and was sticking up straight on top. The other guy, who was standing in Joe's path, was big, too, but with long brown hair, a narrow face, close-set eyes, and a sharp nose and chin. He was twisting a big gold ring on his right hand.

"Well, well," Ricky drawled, giving Frank and Joe a nasty grin. "If it isn't the boy detectives."

Great, Frank thought. So Ricky *does* know.

"Boomer, you should be more careful," Ricky said to the blond. "You don't want to bruise anybody's delicate complexion or ruin anybody's hairstyle, do you?"

Frank saw a look of confusion cross the face of the guy named Boomer. He didn't seem to know how to answer Ricky's question.

Joe said, "You and your buddies are in our way, Ricky. You want to let us by?"

Ricky turned to the rat-faced guy in front of Joe. "Tut, tut, Kenny," he said. "You mustn't make our little friends cross. They might sit down and start bawling."

"Enough clowning," Frank said. "We've got better things to do than listen to this."

"Hey," Boomer said, "you go when we say so, got it?"

"Yeah, that's right," Kenny said. He pointed a finger at Joe, stopping just short of poking him in the chest. Frank saw Joe get into a defensive stance and clench his fists.

Ricky put a hand on each of his buddies' shoulders and said, "Now, now, no rough stuff. Our boy detectives just might decide to holler for some real cops. We don't want that, do we?"

"Cops?" Boomer repeated. "No, we don't need any cops around here. We keep everything real peaceful."

"Come on, Ricky," Frank said firmly. "Let us by."

"Uh-oh," Ricky said, with a mocking grin. "Let the boy detectives go, guys. They're hot on the trail of the crooks! What's the case about—somebody put too much mustard on their hot dog?"

"Listen, Ricky," Joe snapped. "Can the 'boy detective' stuff!"

"Just watch your step," Ricky snapped back. "This isn't your turf, boys. You're poking your noses into matters that are none of your business."

He turned and strode away with his two gorillas at his heels. Joe started after them, fists clenched, but Frank stepped in front of him.

"We'll deal with that jerk later," Frank said firmly. "And we did just learn something. We now know that Ricky *was* listening at the window last night."

"Yeah," Joe said sourly. "And the guy's probably blown our cover to everyone in the show by now."

"Since when did that stop us?" Frank said. "We told Susan we'd help her, cover or not. So let's move it. I want to see what the place is like by daylight."

For the next half hour, Frank and Joe prowled through the fairground. Many of the stands were still closed, but as ten o'clock drew near, the show gradually came to life. At the Italian sausage stand, Joe exchanged greetings with a cheerful woman who was chopping onions and peppers. Across the way at the taco stand, Frank nodded to two men who were cutting tomatoes, lettuce, and cheese while chatting in what sounded like French. The calliope in the center of the merry-go-round gave a preliminary wheeze, then began to grind out a waltz as the wooden horses started to move.

From somewhere near the front gates came a sound like a foghorn. "That must be the signal for opening time," Frank remarked.

He pulled Joe to one side as the four Fratelli Brothers strode up the midway toward the entrance, juggling brightly colored balls and rings. A few moments later, the Hardys saw the first fair-goers appear. Most were families with small children.

"We need to give Susan a progress report. How about if I go and ask her for a list of all the Fairs to Go people at the same time?" Joe suggested suddenly. "That way, we can be sure to talk to everybody who might be of help."

"Good idea," Frank replied. "I'll hang around here until we link up again. And, Joe," he added, "be careful about what you tell Susan about the case. I don't want her acting funny around that nasty stepbrother of hers. We don't want to tip him or anyone else off that we're watching them."

Joe nodded and headed east, in the direction of the trailers. After he'd gone, Frank watched three kids at a game booth across the way. They were trying to toss dimes onto some small squares on a game board. So far, they hadn't done too well, but Frank saw that they were having a great time anyway.

As he watched, Frank tried to plan a strategy for the day. He didn't want Susan to have to suffer through another incident. He wondered if he and his brother could find a way to spook whoever was behind the sabotage and force them out into the open.

The three kids, apparently tired of tossing dimes, started across the midway in the direction of a soft drink stand. As they passed near Frank, he heard a grinding, metallic rumble from nearby.

As he turned to see what was causing it, somebody yelled, "Hey, look out! Heads up!"

Next to the soft drink stand, there were eight steel kegs holding syrup and carbonated water, stacked in two layers on their sides. The stack was collapsing, and the heavy metal barrels were rolling straight at the little group of terrified kids!

6 The Not-So-Fun House

The three kids in the path of the heavy barrels stared at them open-mouthed, frozen in place like deer in a car's headlights. Then they started to scream in fright.

Frank lunged forward, his arms outstretched. He grabbed the kids and pushed them out of the way—and just in time. The first of the barrels struck his left heel as it rumbled past. He stumbled and fell, carrying the three kids with him.

Behind him, he heard more shouts, then a crash. Over his shoulder, he saw that the line of runaway barrels had banged into the game stand across the way. The stand's counter slowly tilted to the left and collapsed.

A crowd was forming as people came running from all directions.

Frank clambered to his feet, then helped the kids up. "Are you okay?" he asked.

One of them—a boy of about eight—was very pale, but he nodded yes. Another, who looked like the little brother of the first, was wiping tears from his cheeks.

"Lisa! Danny! Jeff!" A woman ran up and fell to her knees, embracing the smallest child. "What happened? Are you all right?"

The third, a girl a little older than the others, pointed at Frank and said, "Mom, that guy saved our lives! I thought we were all going to be crushed!"

The woman looked gratefully at Frank. "How can I ever thank you? I only left them for a second to buy some tickets—"

Frank smiled. "I'm just glad I was here," he answered.

The owner of the soft drink stand came running up. "Is everybody all right?" he demanded. "I nearly had a heart attack when I saw the kegs rolling toward you kids. There was no way I could do anything in time, either."

Someone in the crowd said loudly, "These people should be more careful. Somebody could have gotten hurt!"

The guy who ran the game booth came over and grabbed the soft drink concessionaire by the shoulder. "Your kegs wrecked my stand, Augie," he said angrily. "I'm out of business now. What are you going to do about it?"

"Don't worry, Larry, we'll work something out," Augie replied. "I'm just glad nobody got hurt."

Augie turned to the three kids. "Hey, kids, how about some free sodas?" They nodded eagerly. "You, too," he added, giving Frank a grateful look.

Frank followed them over to the stand and waited until the three kids had gotten their drinks and left with their mother. Then he looked at Augie. "What happened? Why did the stack of kegs fall like that?"

"I wish I knew, friend," Augie replied. "It won't happen again, I can promise you that. Excuse me, I'd better get those barrels out of the way before somebody trips over one and decides to sue me."

Frank watched as Augie started rolling the barrels back into place. When the bottom row was full, the concessionaire looked around on the ground, then bent down to pick up a wedge-shaped piece of metal resembling a doorstop.

"Is that what holds them in place?" Frank asked.

"Right," Augie replied. "See, I've got to stack another row on top of this one. The ones on the bottom would start to roll away if I didn't keep them there somehow."

Frank took a closer look. There was a long piece of nylon fishline tied to it. "Is that line supposed to be there?" he asked Augie.

"No, it's not," Augie said in surprise. "It's so clear and thin I didn't notice it. I bet some kid tied it on

51

there for a prank, hoping someone would trip on it. It's a good thing nobody did."

He pulled out a pocketknife and sliced through the knot, then gathered up the fishline and tossed it in a nearby litter basket. Then he went off to get the rest of the kegs.

As soon as Augie turned his back, Frank retrieved the fishline and put it in his pocket. Somebody had obviously pulled out the wedge by tugging on the thin line. And what a coincidence, Frank thought grimly—a piece of fishline had been used for the booby trap setup in the Hardys' yard last night.

Frank looked around, trying to figure out where the culprit had been standing when he pulled on the line. A few feet from the soda booth was a trailer that housed a wheel of fortune. He went around to the back of it and examined the ground. There was a cigarette butt in the dirt. Frank knelt down and picked it up. The brand was a popular one, but it still might be a useful clue—assuming that its presence there wasn't just a coincidence. He took a plastic sandwich bag from his hip pocket and tucked the cigarette inside.

The picture in his mind was pretty clear. Someone had stood there, concealed by the trailer, and used the fishline to pull the wedge out of position, releasing the barrels. But that left one important question unanswered. Had the saboteur acted as soon as there were a lot of people in front of the soft drink stand?

Or had he been waiting specifically for Frank to come in range?

Frank heard a faint noise behind him and spun around. Joe was creeping up on him. "What is it?" Joe whispered. "Are you watching somebody?"

Frank took a deep breath. "No," he replied. In a low voice, he explained what had happened, and showed his brother the cigarette butt.

Joe frowned. "Our trickster is starting to play rougher," he said. "We'd better catch him before somebody really gets hurt."

"Did you find Susan?" Frank asked. "Was she any help?"

"Oh, sure," Joe said with a nod. "It took her a while, but she finally tracked down the list of people who are with Fairs to Go and made a copy for us." He took a folded sheet of paper from his jacket pocket and handed it to Frank.

"You know what I was thinking?" Joe added. "We ought to talk to Morris Tuttle. He probably knows more about the show than anyone, Susan included."

"Good point," Frank replied. "Why don't we split up? You take Tuttle, and I'll see if I can find out what Ricky is up to. I want to figure out why he and his two buddies pulled that stunt this morning. We can meet in front of the Ferris wheel in forty-five minutes and compare notes."

"Check," Joe said. He glanced at his watch. Morris hadn't been in his office earlier when Joe had gone by the trailer to speak to Susan, but he figured Tuttle might have shown up since then.

When Joe reached the trailer and peered through Morris's window, he saw the man sitting at his computer, studying a screenful of numbers. Joe tapped on the glass. Morris looked around quickly, then cleared the screen before getting up to let Joe in.

"What can I do for you?" Tuttle asked as they sat down in his tiny office.

Joe decided on a direct approach. "Do you have any idea who could be trying to wreck Fairs to Go?" he asked. "Or who might have a reason to?"

"As I told Susan yesterday, I haven't ruled out the possibility that we're just having a string of bad luck. But if you want to talk about motives . . ." Morris rubbed his chin. "We like to think we're one big happy family, Joe. But even happy families can have a black sheep or two. And when one family member gets the idea that another is being favored over him, it makes for a lot of bad feeling."

Joe had a hunch as to what Morris was getting at, but he wanted to be sure. "Could you be a little more specific?"

Morris hesitated, then said, "Ricky was very upset when the major asked Susan to manage the show in his place. Ricky feels he's a lot more qualified for the job, especially since Susan's so young."

"Do you think he's right?" Joe asked. "Hasn't he had business school training?"

Morris sniffed. "The best business school for learning how to run a fair is right here, being part of it," he said. "As far as understanding *this* business goes, Susan knows it from the ground up. It's in her blood. The major only married Dora, Ricky's mother, a couple of years ago, and Ricky never spent much time with the show until the major's illness. Besides, it's not just a question of experience. It's a matter of hard work and good business sense."

"Ricky doesn't strike me as a very even-tempered guy," Joe prodded.

"No-o-o . . . The fact is, he's gotten in with an unsavory crowd. He even managed to get two of them onto the fair's payroll."

"Kenny and Boomer," Joe guessed.

"Quite right," Morris said, looking surprised. "You've learned a lot in a hurry, haven't you?"

"We need to, if the show is in as bad shape as Susan thinks," Joe replied. "Just how bad is it, by the way? Is the show really likely to fold?"

"That's highly confidential information," Morris said, a little coolly. "Still, I guess lots of people know by now that we've been losing money steadily for quite a while. And all this talk of a jinx isn't helping matters. Some of the owners of our most profitable concessions have told me they're thinking of signing up with a rival outfit. If that happened, we'd be in a very bad way, obviously. It might come down to a choice between selling the show and closing it."

"Never!"

Morris and Joe looked up. Susan was standing in the doorway.

"Hello, Susan," Morris said calmly. "I didn't hear you come in."

"I know," she retorted. She turned to Joe. "Understand this. My father built Fairs to Go from scratch, and no one—*no one*—is going to destroy it. I'll do whatever it takes to stop them!"

"And we'll do whatever we can to help you do it," Joe said.

After ten minutes of searching, Frank spotted Ricky at the Italian sausage concession. He was leaning over the counter, deep in conversation with a woman in a white apron who seemed to be in charge of the booth.

Frank faded back into the crowd and watched. As Ricky talked, the woman's expression grew more and more unhappy. Finally, she reached down behind the counter, then extended her closed fist to Ricky. With a grin, he took whatever was in it and put it in his pocket. He gave the woman a jaunty salute and walked on to the next booth, which sold cassettes and CDs.

Frank watched as the guy in charge came over and listened to Ricky, then shook his head. Ricky talked to him some more, but once again the answer was a shake of the head.

What were they talking about? Frank wondered as Ricky stalked off, looking angry. The guy in the booth looked angry, too. Frank thought about stopping to ask him about the conversation, but he didn't want to risk losing sight of Ricky.

The same pattern was repeated at the next four booths. Ricky talked to the proprietor, who then either handed him something very secretively or refused. But what were they giving him?

When the woman running the kiddie merry-go-round stretched her hand out to Ricky, Frank found out. As she uncovered her fist, Frank caught a glimpse of green. Money! Ricky took it and stuffed it in his pocket.

The concessionaires were making payoffs to Ricky! But why? Frank wondered. People usually made payoffs in exchange for favors, or because they were being threatened. Ricky had a relationship to the management of the fair and might be able to give special privileges to those on his good side. He also had a couple of sidekicks who looked as if they'd enjoy wrecking a booth or two, to demonstrate what would happen to concessionaires who didn't pay up.

But why would Ricky shake down the people who were so crucial to the success of his stepfather's fair? Frank wondered. And just as important, why hadn't any of the concessionaires blown the whistle on him?

Ricky crossed over to West Avenue and turned left. Frank recognized the soft drink booth where the runaway barrels had almost bowled over the kids. Augie, the proprietor, saw him and nodded. Frank expected Ricky to stop at some of the booths around this area and talk to the proprietors, but he didn't.

He continued straight down the avenue to the Fun House.

The front of the Fun House was an enormous clown face. Its eyes rolled in time to mad laughter that blasted from the loudspeakers. Ricky waved casually to the ticket taker and boarded one of the cars, which carried him through the clown's wide-open mouth into the Fun House.

Frank walked toward the Fun House as quickly as he could without attracting attention. Another car was gliding into place as he reached the entrance. The car had two seats, both facing front and wide enough to hold two people. Frank showed his pass to the ticket taker, who glanced at it and waved him past. Frank jumped into the front seat of the car just as it started toward the clown's mouth.

A moment later, he was in total darkness. To his left, something cackled madly. A flash of light revealed a grinning, dancing skeleton. Frank peered ahead, trying to make out the car Ricky was in. No luck. The flash of light went out, leaving Frank with colored spots dancing before his eyes.

Then the car hurtled around a sharp curve, throwing Frank to one side. There was a sinister baritone laugh, so low and loud that Frank could feel the vibrations in his chest. Something that felt like cobwebs brushed against his face. Glowing green, eerie hands reached out from the darkness, as if to grab him and pull him out of the car.

This Fun House had some pretty spooky special effects, he thought—Joe and Chet would love it.

When something armlike slid around his neck, he was sure this was the spookiest effect of all. Then the arm tightened, and Frank realized suddenly that it wasn't a special effect at all.

Someone had slipped into the backseat of his car and was trying to strangle him!

7 Hose Job

Frank gasped for air and tried to claw at the arm around his throat. As it tightened, he braced his feet against the front railing of the car, arched his back, and thrust himself backward over his seat, in the direction of his attacker. The top of his head smashed into something that yielded. He heard a yelp of pain and felt the arm loosen slightly.

Frank gulped down a deep breath, but before he could take advantage of the new situation, the arm tightened again. He began to see flashes of colored light before his eyes. Gritting his teeth, he grabbed the attacker's arm with both hands and tried to pull it loose. No good. Jerking his body from side to side, he fought convulsively to get another precious lungful of air.

Thinking quickly, Frank shifted his grip to his

attacker's hand. He found the little finger and started to bend it backward. There was another, louder yelp of pain, and the pressure of the arm disappeared.

Panting, Frank jumped to his feet and swung a fist unsuccessfully in his opponent's direction. Unfortunately, the momentum of his punch carried him over the side of the still-moving car. As he landed on the tunnel floor, his feet slipped, and he barely managed to stay upright.

Too late, he realized that the wall of the dark tunnel was only inches away. He slammed into it as the car slid by, scraping against the backs of his thighs and squeezing him against the wall.

Suddenly, Frank spotted a light out of the corner of his eye. When he turned his head to look, he saw an alcove just ahead; and in it was a vampire in full evening dress, complete with white face, red lips, and glittering eyes. The light was coming from a candle it was holding in one hand. Its other hand was reaching toward the shadowy figure of Frank's attacker, who was still in the backseat of his car.

Then the car rounded a curve, and the vampire's candle went out, leaving Frank in darkness once again.

Frank made a rapid choice. If he tried to follow the car in the darkness, he would have very little chance of catching up to it. But what if he tried to head off his attacker? It was worth a shot.

"Fun houses," Frank muttered to himself as he groped his way along the tunnel toward the front entrance. "Are we having fun yet?"

61

The ticket taker gave Frank an astonished look when he ran out of the clown's mouth. "Hey, what are you trying to pull?" he called.

Frank went over to him. "Is there any way to get out of the Fun House without coming past here?" he asked breathlessly.

"Why?" the ticket taker demanded. "What's going on here?"

"A friend is trying to play a joke on me," Frank replied, improvising quickly. "I'd like to turn the tables on him if I can."

"Oh." The man frowned at him. "Well, there's an emergency exit. That's the law in lots of states, you know."

"Where is it?" Frank asked urgently.

"Where?" the ticket taker repeated. "Why, about ten feet past the Bride of Frankenstein, and just before you get to the giant spiderweb."

Frank rolled his eyes impatiently. "No, no, I mean, where does it come out?"

"Oh. Around back. But you can't—"

Frank missed the rest of the sentence. He was off running to the back of the Fun House. He figured Ricky couldn't have been his attacker, since Ricky was in a car in front of him and Frank would have seen him if he'd tried to double back. Ricky must be long gone by now, Frank thought, but I might still be able to corner whoever attacked me.

He was a dozen feet from the back of the building when he heard a door slam, then footsteps pounding away. Frank put on more speed, but by the time he reached the area behind the Fun House, all he saw was a figure vanishing around the corner of the fortune-teller's tent, which was next to the Fun House. He raced after the figure, but whoever it was had already disappeared into the crowd on the bustling avenue.

Just as Frank dashed out into the avenue, someone came out of the fortune-teller's tent. Frank had to stop short to prevent a head-on collision.

It was Joe. "Where have you been, Frank?" he demanded. "I've been looking all over for you!"

"That's a long story," Frank replied. He quickly told his brother about his adventure in the Fun House. "The good news is that we seem to be putting a scare into the bad guys," he concluded. "I just wish we were as hot on their trail as they seem to think we are."

Joe was starting to tell Frank what he had learned from Morris Tuttle when he noticed the four Fratelli Brothers coming in their direction. For once, the clowns were not on stilts, and he could see how tall they were. They were all pretty close in height to the clown who had paid the Hardys a visit the night before.

It could have been any of them, Joe thought.

Frank seemed to have the same idea. "Hey, guys, do you have a minute?" he called to the clowns.

"We have lots of minutes," the clown with the punk hairdo replied. "Sixty of them every hour."

Another one laughed and squeezed his large round red nose. It let out a loud honk.

"Can we talk to you?" Frank persisted.

"You already are," the first clown said. "Hey, do you know where Napoleon kept his armies?"

Without thinking, Joe ventured, "In France?"

"No, he kept his armies in his sleevies!"

All four clowns cracked up. When the guffaws started to die down, the one with the red nose said, "What did the porcupine say to the cactus?"

The one with the punk hairdo answered, "Is that you, Ma?"

Joe rolled his eyes. The four clowns would obviously keep this up all day, if he let them. "Look," he said, shouting over their laughter, "the thing is, after we left the show last night and went back to town, we passed somebody in a clown costume and makeup on the street. A friend of mine swore it was one of you guys. I bet him it wasn't."

A third clown, in whiteface and baggy pants, said, "You win. How much of a cut do we get?"

"We didn't put money on it," Joe replied quickly. "Still, I don't know if my friend will just take my word for it. Are you sure none of you went into town last night after the show?"

"Sure, we're sure," the one with the punk hairdo said. "We had our regular Saturday night card game after the show. And we were all there, so how could we have been in town?"

"Yesterday was Friday," Frank pointed out. "Not Saturday."

The clown shrugged. "So? Sometimes we have our

Saturday night card game on Friday night instead. Big deal."

"Do most of the people with Fairs to Go know about your Saturday night card games?" Frank asked.

"Sure. Most of the people in the show have sat in on them at least once," the clown in whiteface replied.

"Did you tell a lot of people that you were switching it to Friday this week?" Frank continued.

The one in whiteface glanced at the others before saying, "We decided at closing time, and we just told each other. What about it?"

Joe said, "Maybe the clown we saw was hoping people would think he was one of you guys. You're pretty well known, after all."

"The word's 'famous,'" the one in whiteface said.

"Or 'celebrated,'" the one with the red nose added. "Did this clown you saw try to cash a check or anything?"

Before Frank or Joe could answer, the fourth clown, who was wearing a torn tuxedo and a battered top hat with a big flower pinned to the side, said, "You know who these guys are? They're the two detectives Ricky told us about."

Joe and Frank exchanged a glance.

"Wow, can I see your magnifying glass?" the clown in whiteface asked the Hardys. The other clown honked his nose once again.

"Look, this is serious," Frank started to say.

"We're wasting our coffee break on you guys," the one in the tuxedo said. "And that *is* serious."

65

As if on cue, all four of them walked away. After two steps, they went into a synchronized series of cartwheels that carried them around the corner and out of sight.

"That was pretty useless," Joe observed.

"Not entirely," Frank replied. "We did learn that they have an alibi for each other for last night. Either they're all lying, or the guy we saw was someone else, disguised as a clown."

Joe said, "And here comes candidate number one."

Frank looked over his shoulder. Ricky was approaching them with a big grin on his face.

"Hey, look who's here," he said in a mocking voice. "Are you guys having fun playing detective? Maybe you should give the Fun House a try. There's all kinds of scary stuff in there."

Frank took a deep breath, counted to ten, then said, "We're just trying to help, Ricky. Fairs to Go is in trouble. I would think you'd want to give us any cooperation you could—unless you're the one who's causing the problem."

"The one who's causing the problem is my dear stepsister, Susan," Ricky retorted. "This is a big, complicated operation. It takes somebody with a firm hand and a lot of business knowledge to keep it on track. Susan's just a kid. Sure, she knows her way around the show, but she doesn't have what it takes to run it."

"Do you?" Frank asked evenly.

"You bet I do," Ricky replied, sticking his chin out. "And sooner or later, the major is going to realize it.

He'd better. Otherwise, Morris Tuttle will end up owning Fairs to Go before the year is out."

"Morris?" Joe repeated. "What do you mean?"

Ricky raised his eyebrows. "Dear Susan didn't tell you? Morris offered to buy out the major's share of FTG. That would make him the sole owner. Not that the major's share is worth that much these days, with the show losing money so fast. Still, if things go on this way, the major might decide that cash in the hand is a better deal than half of nothing. And nothing's what he'll end up with, if Susan stays in charge."

"Business will pick up," Joe asserted, "once we catch the person who's trying to wreck the show."

"You turkeys?" Ricky scoffed. "What a laugh. But go ahead, waste your time. Maybe a couple more clowns are just what FTG needs to be a big success." Ricky turned on his heel and walked away.

"Did you hear that?" Joe demanded angrily.

"Sure," Frank replied. "He was trying to get us riled. The way he told us to go to the Fun House, he might as well have admitted he had something to do with that attack on me. And why do you think he mentioned clowns at the end? Because he, or one of his buddies, planted that bomb at our house last night, that's why."

"Then what are we waiting for? Let's grab him," Joe said.

Frank shook his head. "We don't have any real proof," he pointed out.

Joe took a deep breath. "Okay, you're right," he admitted. "We shouldn't jump to conclusions. But what about the story that Morris offered to buy the major's share of the show? Why would he do that if the show's in such terrible shape?"

"His partner just had a heart attack and probably needs money," Frank said. "Maybe it's Morris's way of helping out without making it look like charity. Or maybe he thinks he can turn it around if he's in charge. Still, I don't trust anything Ricky says. I'd like to check it out with Susan. Let's go see if she's in her office."

Frank and Joe walked across the fairground toward the trailers and the carnival workers motor homes. But they found Susan's office dark.

"We can try again later," Frank said, turning away. Suddenly his foot caught on something. A second later, he was flat on the ground.

Joe rushed over to help him. "What happened?"

Frank pointed to a garden hose stretched across the path. "Who left a hose here? I'm lucky I didn't break my neck."

As he lifted the hose, Frank felt it vibrating. "Hey, that's odd," he said. "The water's turned on. I don't remember any gardens around here."

He and Joe found the source of the hose. It was attached to a faucet, which was turned on full force. The Hardys traced the hose back the other way and saw that it went through a jagged hole in the window of Tuttle's office at the end of the trailer.

"Come on, we've got to get in there!" Frank shouted. He raced around the corner of the trailer with Joe at his heels just as Susan walked up to the trailer and pulled the door open.

"Susan, don't go in there!" Frank shouted. But it was too late.

Susan screamed as water came pouring out the door. She staggered back off the step, slipped on a patch of slick mud, and fell backward, smashing her head on the ground. One loud groan, then she was silent.

8 Tunnel of Terror

Joe and Frank rushed over to Susan. As Joe knelt down in the mud next to her, Frank warned, "Don't move her—she may be injured."

Susan opened her eyes and blinked, then raised her head. Joe put his hand to her forehead, and said, "Lie down. You've been injured."

"No, I'm okay," she said in a shaky voice. "I'm just a little dizzy, that's all."

"Joe's right, though. You'd better lie still," Frank said.

"All that water—where did it come from?" she asked, pushing herself up on one elbow. Most of the water had emptied out of the trailer and been absorbed in the mud, but there was still a trickle coming from the doorway.

"Somebody stuck a hose through the office window and turned it on," Joe explained.

"That reminds me—I'll be right back," Frank murmured, and headed toward the faucet.

"They flooded my office?" Susan said in outrage. "I've got to see!"

She started to get up, then fell back. Joe caught her. "Hey, take it easy," he said.

Frank returned, with Morris following, his gray hair disheveled.

"Susan," Morris called out, rushing to her side. "Frank just told me what happened. Are you all right? Should we call a doctor?"

"No, I'm okay," she replied. "But I can't say the same about the office. What if water got into the files?"

"Files?" Morris repeated in an alarmed voice. "Files? Oh, no—the computer!"

He rushed into the trailer. A moment later, Joe heard a cry from inside.

"Help me up," Susan said urgently to Joe. "I've got to know the worst."

Joe and Frank supported Susan up the step to the trailer door, then followed her inside. They squelched across the water-soaked carpet. Morris was standing in his tiny office, staring down at a blank computer monitor.

"The system's a total loss," he said grimly. "The water must have been aimed straight at it. Everything that could short-circuit did. I'm surprised there wasn't an electrical fire."

71

"Was the computer on?" Frank asked.

Morris nodded. "I turn it on first thing in the morning, and it stays on until bedtime. What a mess. I don't know what we'll do now."

Susan took a deep breath and said, "We'll find the money to buy another computer. Tomorrow, if we can locate a computer store that's open on Sunday."

"You don't understand," Morris replied. "It's not the computer I'm worried about. All our records for the past eight months were on the hard disk. Now they're gone, forever."

"What about backups?" Frank said.

Morris sighed. "I know you're always supposed to back up your hard drive. But I'm afraid I'm like practically everyone else—too lazy to do it, except once in a while. Besides, who'd expect something like this to happen?"

"Morris, are you telling me that we've lost all the financial records for Fairs to Go?" Susan said, her voice rising with anxiety. "Everything was on the computer?"

"Just about," he said soberly. "I did print out a fairly detailed summary just three days ago. I wanted to show it to your father. But the original records are gone. I'm sorry, Susan. It's all my fault."

"I can't believe it!" Susan moaned. "What'll we do now?"

"Find whoever broke the window, stuck the hose in, and turned it on," Joe said. "And don't worry, Susan, we will. We're hot on their trail."

"Joe's right," Frank added. "The people who are

trying to wreck Fairs to Go are obviously getting desperate."

"Are you getting anywhere?" Susan pleaded. "Have you learned anything new since we talked this morning, Joe?"

"We've got lots of ideas," Joe replied, although he didn't feel as confident as he sounded. So far, he and Frank had plenty of suspects but not a single solid clue.

"How can I help? Please tell me," Susan said.

"Don't give up hope," Frank replied. "And don't let the crooks see that they're getting you down. Hanging on to your confidence is half the battle. Now, we'd better get back to work."

"We have work to do, too," Susan sighed, looking around the waterlogged office. Morris nodded grimly. "Thank you, both of you," Susan added. "I really appreciate your help."

"You're sure you're okay?" Joe asked worriedly.

Susan managed a smile. "I'm fine. Really."

As he and Frank walked back toward the midway, Joe said, "Trouble is, we really haven't been that much help to Susan." He looked at his brother. "We never did ask her about Morris Tuttle wanting to buy her out, you know."

"It hardly seemed the time, especially with Morris standing right there," Frank pointed out. "Anyway, I don't really see Morris as a suspect. I can't believe he'd go so far as to destroy his own office *and* an expensive computer system, just to make the sabotage look real."

Joe shrugged. "Well, we have enough suspects without adding him to the list, that's for sure. Too many, in fact. I think we need some help on this case ourselves."

"I was thinking the same thing," Frank replied. "I wonder what Chet's got lined up for tomorrow."

"Let's find out," said Joe.

Five minutes later, Frank turned from a pay phone and gave Joe the thumbs-up. "He'll do it," he reported.

"What do we have to give him?" Joe asked. "A year's supply of souvlaki sandwiches?"

Frank grinned. "Nope, we got off cheap. A couple of rides on the bumper cars—but I had to promise that we'd do it along with him!"

On the way to the fairground the next morning, the guys divided up tailing assignments. Chet took Raoul, the former strongman, Joe chose Farkas, and Frank stayed with Ricky.

"We'll have to be very careful about being noticed," Frank said as they walked through the entrance. "Look how empty the place is now. The crowds probably won't start showing up until after lunch."

"Lunch . . ." Chet repeated.

"Down, boy," Joe teased. "You just had breakfast."

"Why don't we all meet in an hour at the bumper cars?" Frank suggested. "We can compare notes and have a little fun at the same time.

"Uh-oh," he added in a changed voice. "Duty calls—I just spotted Ricky. Catch you guys later."

After fifteen minutes of shadowing Ricky, Frank was almost sure that he was on the right trail. Once again, Susan's stepbrother was making the rounds, stopping at each concession to talk to the owner. Again, some proprietors gave him something and others refused.

Eventually, Ricky reached the Ferris wheel and started talking to Althea. Frank watched from behind the corner of the shooting gallery, twenty feet away. Althea had her chin up and her shoulders back, and shook her head when Ricky finished talking. Althea folded her arms in front of her and said something that made Ricky visibly angry. Then Ricky spat some nasty words back, which Frank couldn't hear. Only after Ricky had left did Althea let her guard down, and Frank saw she was upset.

Frank decided to seize the moment and talk to her, rather than continue to follow Ricky. "Trouble?" he asked, coming up to her.

Althea's face was expressionless. "What can I do for you?" she asked coolly.

Frank decided to be totally direct. "You can tell me what Ricky wants from you," he replied.

A look of surprise flashed in her dark eyes. "I don't know what you're talking about."

"I saw him here with you," Frank told her. "And I saw how upset you looked. Hey, I want to help you."

Frank's plea didn't work. "We were talking about

75

the show, that's all. How things are going, stuff like that." Althea looked away. "Excuse me, I'm busy."

Frank looked around. No one seemed interested in the Ferris wheel.

"Althea?" Frank said. "The show's in trouble. You know that. And you can do something about it."

She whirled around. "You, too?" she said bitterly. "Which horse are you backing, and for how much?"

"I don't understand," Frank said, confused. When she was silent, he decided to lay all his cards on the table. "Susan asked me and my brother to help her find out who is trying to wreck Fairs to Go. I know that's not what we said yesterday, but it's true. Ask her."

"So that's it. I thought you were too full of questions to be students," Althea said with a sideways glance.

"What did you mean about which horse I'm backing?" Frank persisted.

"Nothing," Althea mumbled.

"What you know may help us save the show," Frank said, pressing her. "I'm not asking you to go out on a limb. Just tell me what Ricky wanted from you."

Althea stared at the ground for what seemed like a long time. Finally she looked up and met Frank's eyes. "I don't want to talk here," she said softly. "Let me think . . . oh, I know."

She called out to her assistant. "Dave? Take over, will you? I'll be back in ten minutes." To Frank, she said, "Come with me. I know where we can talk in private."

To Frank's surprise, she led him to the Tunnel of Love. She waved to the attendant and called, "How about sending us around, Vic?"

"Sure thing," Vic called back. "No business yet today, anyway."

Frank sat down beside Althea in a swan-shaped carriage that ran on narrow rails. It glided through a heart-shaped opening into a dark tunnel. The darkness was relieved by twinkling lights in many colors and flashes of strobe lights revealing paintings of famous couples—Romeo and Juliet, Antony and Cleopatra, Elizabeth Taylor and Richard Burton— strolling hand in hand. Frank heard distant strains of music and coughed as they passed through a mist of perfume.

"About Ricky—" he said, growing impatient with Althea's silence.

Althea took a deep breath. "I've had problems with him since the first day we met," she said. "He's got the idea that just being the major's stepson is enough to make him an important person, and he's fond of throwing his weight around. I don't want to be unfair. Maybe he really does want what's best for the show and thinks that Susan's going to drive it into the ground. All the same, this new scheme of his—hey, what's that?"

Frank saw Althea become rigid with tension, and whipped his head around to face front. Somewhere up ahead, what looked like a match flared to life, then suddenly went out. It was followed by a shower of yellow sparks.

The sparks illuminated the walls of the narrow tunnel and revealed the dim shape of someone with a weirdly flattened face. Frank stared. He was sure it wasn't part of the show. Someone with a nylon stocking pulled down over his head was waiting to ambush them.

The yellow sparks disappeared, and Frank peered into the darkness. Suddenly a ball of green flame came blasting down the tunnel, straight toward him and Althea.

9 The Mystery Driver

"Get down!" Frank shouted as the fireball whooshed toward them. He flung himself sideways, on top of Althea, and crooked his arm to protect his face.

The green ball of flame passed just inches over the swan boat. Moments later a red fireball followed it. This one grazed the swan's head and exploded in a shower of sparks. One spark seared the back of Frank's neck. As he slapped at it frantically, he heard running footsteps retreating down the tunnel. Another ball of flame—this one acid blue—struck the tunnel wall and fell to the floor.

"I think he's gone," Frank said, sitting up and peering over the front of the swan. He debated whether to chase the guy, but decided that it was too late.

"I just figured out what that was—a Roman candle," he continued. "Plenty scary, but not very dangerous."

Althea pushed herself upright. "It sure scared me," she admitted.

Frank touched the tiny burn on his neck gingerly. "It's painful, too, if it hits you," he said.

"I never imagined—" Althea began. Then she stopped abruptly.

"What?" Frank asked.

"Nothing," she said. "This is all my fault, for deciding to come here."

"You know who attacked us, don't you?" Frank said slowly. "Or at least you have a very good idea."

"How could I? That's ridiculous," Althea replied.

Frank ran through the major suspects in his mind. Ricky, Farkas, Ricky's two henchmen . . . and then there was Althea's jealous admirer, Raoul. He might easily have been driven to extremes if he saw her and Frank entering the Tunnel of Love together.

"You told me that your friend Raoul helps out wherever he can," he said. "Does he have anything to do with the nightly fireworks display?"

In the dim light of the tunnel, Althea eyed him closely, then said, "Yes. He's one of two crew members who set it up and set it off. But that doesn't mean—"

The swan boat was nearing the end of the ride. Frank said quickly, "Don't worry, I won't jump to conclusions. Now, you had something to tell me about

Ricky. We don't have much time. What was it? What is this scheme of his?"

"Nothing," Althea said, shaking her head.

"What do you mean, nothing?" Frank protested. "You brought me here so you could tell me."

"I changed my mind," she said, as the swan glided out into the daylight. "Excuse me, I've got a business to run."

A frustrated Frank watched Althea climb out of the swan boat and hurry off in the direction of the Ferris wheel.

Frank sighed, then climbed out of the swan boat slowly. The case was becoming murkier by the moment. *Someone* had aimed that Roman candle at him and Althea in the Tunnel of Love. The obvious suspect was her jealous admirer, Raoul. He had means—access to the fireworks—as well as motive. But if Raoul were responsible, why would that make Althea decide not to talk to Frank about Ricky's schemes?

Frank hadn't recognized their attacker's face, distorted as it was by the stocking. But maybe Althea had—she knew everyone at Fairs to Go much better than he. Did she suspect, or even know for sure, that it was Ricky who had mounted the attack as a warning to her? Or if not Ricky, then one of his henchmen?

There was an easy way to check up on Raoul, at least. Chet was keeping an eye on him. Frank glanced at his watch, then turned in the direction of the bumper car concession, where Chet and Joe were supposed to meet him soon.

Joe was hiding behind a large toolbox in a narrow aisle by the merry-go-round. He straightened up and rubbed a sore spot in the small of his back, then crouched down again. Patience is an important ingredient in successful detective work, he told himself for the tenth time. But would it pay off here?

His assignment was to watch Farkas, and that was exactly what he had been doing, for almost an hour. During that time, Farkas had dealt with about a dozen clients. Naturally, nobody won anything—obviously, the fix was still on.

Farkas walked over to a refreshment stand to buy a cup of coffee. When he finished, he tossed the empty container into the middle of the walkway, even though there was a litter basket just a few feet away. Nice guy, Joe thought.

Suddenly, a weirdly elongated shadow appeared on the ground next to Joe. He jumped up and turned, just in time to collide with the stilt-walking clown with the punk hairdo and black leather outfit. The nine-foot-tall clown swayed wildly back and forth before he finally caught his balance.

"What do you think you're doing?" the clown demanded loudly, glaring down at Joe.

"Please, I'm busy," Joe said, as softly as he could. He glanced over his shoulder, worried that Farkas had spotted him. He started to crouch behind the toolbox again, but then the other three Fratelli Brothers appeared in the narrow aisle.

"Well, look who's here. It's the detective!" one of them said in a loud voice.

"Shhh!" Joe said desperately. The situation was turning into a nightmare.

"Shall we dance?" the clown in the torn tuxedo said. He extended a white-gloved hand to take Joe's arm. Joe pulled away.

"Listen, guys, I'm really very busy now," he pleaded. "Why don't you go play somewhere else?"

"He doesn't appreciate us," the clown in whiteface complained.

"It's not that," Joe began. He glanced across the walkway and clenched his jaw. In the instant that the clowns had distracted him from his task, someone he didn't know had stepped behind the counter of the shooting gallery. And Farkas? Joe looked around wildly and saw him hurrying away, tucking an envelope into the pocket of his plaid suit.

"Look, I've got to go," Joe said to the clowns. "Really!"

In response, the stilt-walking clowns formed a ring around him. As they circled, they chanted, "Play with us! Play with us!"

Joe *had* to follow Farkas! He didn't know what that envelope contained, but his instincts told him that it might be a vital clue. He saw an opening and ducked through the ring. He hoped the clowns wouldn't come after him. How could he possibly tail someone unnoticed if he had four nine-feet-tall clowns tagging along?

Joe stayed as far back as he dared, as Farkas walked quickly across the fairground and into the trailer park. The shooting gallery operator went straight to a large blue-and-yellow tent. As he lifted the flap of the entrance, Joe caught a glimpse of a folding table and chairs, and deduced that this was the cafeteria tent for employees of the fair. Apparently Farkas was having an early lunch.

A long one, too. Twenty minutes later, Joe was still hovering near the mess tent. He was due to meet Frank and Chet at the bumper car rink, but he couldn't give up now. Other members of the fair's crew had entered the tent, and some of them had come out again, but there was still no sign of Farkas. A horrible suspicion seized Joe. Could Farkas have given him the slip?

He strode over to the mess tent and pushed inside. At the back was a long table with a salad bar, hot dishes on food warmers, and a coffee urn. At a smaller table not far from the entrance were four guys eating lunch, including Carl, the foreman of the fair's work crew. There was no sign of Farkas.

Joe was so angry that he didn't even notice Carl waving to him. Fooled by one of the oldest tricks in the book! Farkas must have come into the tent, then left by the back exit. Coincidence? Or had he done it deliberately? Either way, he was long gone.

Joe strode over to Carl's table and asked, "Have you seen Farkas?"

Carl glanced over his shoulder. "He was here a while ago," he replied. "I guess he split. You might try his booth. You know where it is?"

"I know," Joe said. "Only too well," he muttered under his breath.

As he left the mess tent, he took another look at his watch. His appointment to meet Frank and Chet at the bumper cars had been for ten minutes earlier. What better way than bumper cars to work off some of his anger over Farkas giving him the slip?

Joe found Frank and Chet at the ticket booth for the bumper cars.

"So Raoul could have slipped away long enough to attack us?" Frank was asking Chet.

"I guess so," Chet said, suddenly very interested in the tips of his shoes.

"Attack who?" Joe demanded. "How? When?"

"I'll tell you in a minute," Frank replied.

"Look, I couldn't follow him everywhere," Chet burst out. "He would have spotted me. But he wasn't out of my sight for more than four or five minutes, I can tell you that."

Frank's eyes flashed with annoyance. "Then what matters is whether they were the right four or five minutes, and we don't really have any way of knowing." He turned to Joe and briefly described the Roman candle attack in the Tunnel of Love.

"Were either of you hurt?" Joe asked quickly.

"No, fortunately," Frank replied.

"That's good." Joe cleared his throat. "It sounds as if we've all had a bad morning. Farkas just gave me the slip." He filled them in on what had happened at the mess tent.

"Hey, don't let it get you down," Frank said. "By now, everybody with the show must know who we are and what we're trying to do here. Maybe it's better that way. If anybody knows something and wants to help, at least they know to come to us."

"And if they know something and *don't* want to help, they know to steer clear of us," Joe said grimly. "I feel like bashing something. Who's ready for bumper cars?"

"Me," Chet said promptly. "And I hope you're in good shape. I'm planning to trade bashes with you two for one."

Tickets in hand, the three guys lined up at the chain with the other customers and waited for the next break between rounds. When it came, they scrambled to grab the cars they wanted. Joe's was bright green, Frank's red, and Chet's bright yellow.

The current came on. Joe floored his car and aimed it toward the far end of the track. Just as he picked up speed, someone slammed into his left rear side, spinning his car sideways. As he cranked the wheel to the right to straighten out, he heard Chet's triumphant voice, "Gotcha! That's one!"

"Then you've got two coming to you," Joe shouted back. With a growl, Joe straightened out and pushed the Go button as far as he could. There was a burst of static from overhead, where the commutator touched the electrified ceiling, and the car started moving. As

Chet was just rounding the far curve Joe plowed straight into the side of his car. Joe backed off in time to avoid a little girl's attempt to ram him head-on, then sped off after Frank.

Joe was racing down the straightaway when, out of the corner of his eye, he caught sight of a familiar plaid suit. Farkas! The shooting gallery owner was walking by the bumper car entrance, glancing over his shoulder, as if making sure no one was following him. He didn't look inside the bumper car rink.

Watching Farkas, Joe forgot where he was and took his foot off the accelerator. A moment later, a car smashed into him from behind, knocking him into a tangle of parked cars.

"Number two!" Chet cried as he maneuvered past.

Joe ignored him. This time, he wasn't going to lose Farkas. He jumped out of the bumper car and began to hurry across the floor toward the exit.

"Hey, you," a voice boomed over the PA system. "Get back in your car! You're going to get run over!"

Joe paused to let a little pack of cars pass. Frank was so startled to see Joe that he spun his steering wheel and rammed into the wall. Moments later, another kid rammed into him. Joe jumped back, out of danger, then started across the track again.

He was nearing the outer edge of the floor when some sixth sense warned him of danger. He looked back over his shoulder.

A blue bumper car had just rounded the turn and was starting to pick up speed. Its driver had on a red baseball cap pulled low over his face, sunglasses, and a big gold ring on his right hand. His bushy black mustache looked totally bogus.

Joe realized that the guy was steering his bumper car straight at him. And there was no room to dodge. In another moment, Joe would be crushed between the onrushing car and the wall just behind him.

10 Hey, Rube!

Joe tried to back away from the speeding bumper car, but the wall was in his way. And from the top of the wall to the ceiling, there was a wire net. Its purpose was to keep people from entering the rink without a ticket, but right now, it was also keeping Joe from getting *out* of the rink by jumping the wall. He was trapped, and the blue car was less than a dozen feet away now.

Unless . . . Joe recalled some moves from a gymnastics class he had taken. Without wasting another second, he put his hands behind him, flat on the top of the waist-high wall, then bent his arms and crouched slightly. He waited until the bumper car was almost upon him. Then with all his force, he thrust himself upward, straightening his arms and swinging his legs up parallel to the floor, well above the level of the bumper car.

The blue car slammed into the wall just below him. The wall shook violently under Joe's hands. Joe kicked out with his feet, aiming them at the head of his assailant. The man dodged, but Joe's left foot grazed his face, knocking off the fake mustache. Before Joe could register his features, though, the man spun the wheel of the bumper car and sped off down the track.

For one moment, Joe was tempted to run after him, but decided it would be too dangerous.

Chet and Frank came speeding over. "What happened?" Frank demanded. "Are you okay?"

Joe pointed at the retreating bumper car. "You see the guy in the red cap?" he said. "Don't lose him. He tried to run me down."

Not waiting for a reply, Joe ran along the wall to the exit and hurried in the direction that Farkas had taken. He was passing the fortune-teller's tent when he spotted the plaid suit about fifty feet ahead, on the other side of a little knot of fair-goers. Joe pushed his way through the crowd, but Farkas glanced over his shoulder and saw him. A malevolent look came over his face, and he began to walk faster.

Joe went after him. Soon he had closed the gap. He was just reaching out to tap Farkas on the shoulder when the shooting gallery operator suddenly fell to the ground in the middle of the walkway and started shouting, "Hey, Rube! Hey, Rube!"

Joe hesitated, confused. Then he started to reach out and help Farkas up.

"Keep your hands to yourself!" an angry voice growled behind him.

Joe looked around. What he saw made his heart beat faster. In moments, a crowd of angry-looking carnies had materialized, seemingly from nowhere, and were advancing upon him. Beyond them, the fair-goers were backing away from the thickening atmosphere of violence.

Joe stood still, hoping that his unaggressive posture would keep the mob from jumping him. From the menacing looks on their faces, though, he doubted if it would.

He was on the point of trying to break through the ring and run for safety when he heard a gruff voice: "Get up off the ground, Farkas. What's the problem here?"

Joe looked around. Carl, the foreman, was pushing through the circle.

"This civilian came after me, grabbed me, and knocked me down," Farkas said loudly, pointing an angry finger at Joe. Farkas stood up and brushed off his clothes. "He tried to rob me. He knew I was on my way to put my day's receipts in the office safe."

Farkas reached into the inside pocket of his jacket and showed the crowd an envelope, opening it to reveal a stack of bills. As he shoved it back in his pocket, Joe caught a glimpse of the penciled letters R.D. on the front of the envelope.

"That won't wash, Farkas," Carl said. "I saw the whole thing. He didn't grab you, you took a dive."

"Maybe I tripped," Farkas said sullenly. "But he was after me, all right. Why, if he didn't mean to rob me?"

"I just wanted to ask you some questions," Joe said mildly. "But you rushed away before I could even get started. I didn't know I looked so scary. Or maybe I need to change my mouthwash."

Everybody laughed, and the tension drained away. Farkas looked around. Apparently realizing that he had just lost the crowd's support, he said, "Okay, so maybe I made a mistake. It happens. Now bug off, I'm busy." He pushed through the knot of people and hurried away.

Joe wanted to follow, but Carl grabbed his arm. "I don't know what this is about," he said tightly, "but I hope you do. Next time, I might not be on the spot to smooth things over."

"Thanks for your help," Joe replied. "I really appreciate it. But why did everybody come at me like that?"

"Carny tradition," Carl replied. "When a carny calls 'Hey, Rube,' it means he's got trouble. So everybody pitches in to deal with the problem. Road shows and fairs always attract a few wise guys and troublemakers. You can't call the cops every time it happens, so we handle our hassles ourselves.

"Just watch yourself," Carl concluded. "The last thing FTG needs at this point is more trouble."

After he'd gone, Joe hurried off in the direction

that Farkas had taken, but there was no sign of the plaid suit. Muttering to himself, Joe returned to the bumper car concession. Chet and Frank were waiting by the entrance.

"Where did you go?" Frank asked him. "Are you all right?"

Joe explained, and added, "Did you get a good look at the guy who tried to run me down?"

"The one in the cap and shades?" Chet replied. "Nope. Sorry. We tried to catch up to him, but the rink was too crowded, and he got away."

Joe slapped his fist into his palm. "Another dead end," he complained. "If only I'd gotten a better look at his face after I knocked his mustache off!"

"Well, we know it wasn't Farkas," Frank pointed out. "And Raoul is probably too big to fit into a bumper car. What about Ricky?"

Joe considered the possibility for a moment, then shook his head. "I don't think so. Ricky has all those acne scars on his face. I think I would have noticed them."

At that moment, a girl walked by wearing gold hoop earrings. "Wait a minute, I just remembered," Joe exclaimed. "The guy was wearing a big gold ring on his right hand."

"Kenny!" Frank exclaimed. "I noticed his ring yesterday. That figures. We should have known that Ricky wouldn't do his own dirty work, as long as he has those two cavemen to do it for him."

"I'm getting confused," Chet said. "You're saying that Ricky's the one who's trying to wreck the show?"

"The evidence is beginning to pile up that way," Frank replied. "Maybe he thinks that if the situation gets bad enough, the major will decide that Susan can't handle managing Fairs to Go and turn it over to him."

"Assuming that he and his two buddies are behind all the dirty tricks," Chet continued, "they're trying to stop you—*us*—because they're afraid of being exposed. Is that it?"

"Probably so," Frank said.

Chet scratched his head. "Then where does Farkas come into it? And what about that guy I was supposed to keep an eye on earlier—Raoul?"

"Er—" Frank began.

"Wait," Joe said, interrupting him. "That envelope full of cash that Farkas was carrying. He said he was just taking it to the safe, but the initials on it were R. D. Ricky Delgado!"

Frank clapped him on the shoulder. "Good thinking," he said. "Now we need to figure out *why* Farkas would be giving Ricky money. Not to mention the other concessionaires. Some kind of extortion scheme still seems like the strongest possibility."

"And Raoul?" Chet asked again. "How does he fit in?"

"Well, we know he's jealous of any guy who goes near Althea," Joe said slowly. "And we now know that he has access to fireworks, so he could have planted that bomb at our house the other night. As for what motive he might have to wreck the show, though, I'm not sure."

"He could be working for somebody else," Frank said thoughtfully. "Ricky, for instance, or a rival show. And there's something else, too. Everybody treats Raoul as if he's got muscles where his brains should be. But what if they're wrong? What better cover could he have?"

"What's that about rival shows?" Chet asked. "Couldn't they be behind all this trouble?"

"It's still a possibility," Frank said. "Look, one thing is clear. Whether it's Ricky Delgado or someone else who's trying to ruin Fairs to Go, they're obviously following some plan. We have a much better chance of understanding—and destroying—that plan if we know more about the carny business.

"I'd like to drop by the office and see if Susan is around," Frank went on. "She might be able to tell us something about the fair's competitors. Which ones stand to gain the most if the show goes under? Is there anyone with Fairs to Go who used to be connected to a rival show?"

"Okay," Chet said. "And I'll go back to watching Raoul."

"Good thought," Frank said.

As the three guys crossed the fairground, Joe heard the brass band strike up. He knew what that meant. Sure enough, he saw up ahead, over the heads of the crowd, the gyrating forms of the four Fratelli Brothers.

The clowns were juggling an assortment of objects: a two-liter soda bottle, a claw hammer, a salami, a golf club, and a large rubber fish. The one with the punk

95

haircut noticed Joe, Frank, and Chet. Still juggling, he began to edge through the crowd in their direction.

"Let's get out of here," Joe muttered, "before they make us part of their act."

He started to back away, with Frank right beside him. But Chet didn't act fast enough. Before he could move, he found himself with a rubber fish in his arms. As the crowd laughed and cheered, the clown began herding Chet into the center of the circle. Each time he tried to get away, the clown poked him with the salami. Chet's expression grew increasingly desperate. Then one of the clowns tossed a plastic ring in his direction. In a flash, Chet threw the rubber fish toward the clown and caught the ring. The spectators cheered.

"It's a good thing Chet knows how to juggle," Frank murmured to Joe. "Do we stage a rescue? Or leave him to his fate?"

"Duty first," Joe replied. "We'd better split before they rope us in, too."

As they circled the rear of the crowd, they heard Chet calling, "Frank, Joe, come back here! You'll pay for this, you bums!"

As Joe and Frank neared Susan's office in the trailer park, they heard the unmistakable sound of a woman crying. It was coming from the trailer's open window.

Joe went inside first. As he entered, he noted that most of the water damage had already been taken care of.

Inside, Susan was slumped over her desk with her hands covering her face.

"What is it?" Joe demanded. "What's wrong?"

Susan slowly raised her head, brushing away tears with the back of her hand. Without a word, she picked up a piece of paper from the desk and held it out. Frank stepped forward and took it.

Under the logo of a well-known bank, the computer-generated letter announced that the Fairs to Go account was seriously overdrawn. The company's line of credit was exhausted, and no further checks would be honored. The last paragraph gave a telephone number to call, "to arrange to correct the situation without delay."

"We have a payroll to meet in three days," Susan said in a shaky voice. "I don't know how we'll do it. But unless we do, we're finished. Fairs to Go is going nowhere. It'll kill my dad, but I don't see any way out. We'll either have to shut down or sell the show."

11 Joe's Discovery

"Don't worry, Susan," Joe said quickly. "Your problems are in good hands. You'll pull through."

Frank read the bank letter once again. "When did you get this?" he asked.

"Just now," Susan replied. "Why?"

Frank tapped the paper with his forefinger. "It's dated four days ago. Besides, today's Sunday— there's no mail delivery."

"It probably came yesterday, then," Susan said. "Morris must not have shown it to me right away because he was trying to find some way to straighten out the situation. Does it really matter?"

"It might," Frank said.

Susan shook her head. "Look, I really appreciate the way you've tried to help. It was really sweet of you, and I won't ever forget it. But it's no good. I can't fight this any longer."

"Hey, this is no time to give up," Frank replied. "We're getting close to a solution."

"Frank's right," Joe said. "When did you say the payroll is due? Three days from now? That gives us plenty of time to solve the case."

"I can't ask you—" she began.

"You don't have to," Joe said, breaking in. "We're offering. Right, Frank?"

"Absolutely," Frank said. He grabbed one of the folding chairs, pulled it up to the desk, and sat down facing Susan. "There's a lot we haven't had time to learn yet. For instance, how does an operation like this make money?"

"It doesn't," Susan said bitterly. "Didn't you read that letter from the bank?"

"What I mean is," Frank said patiently, "where does the income for Fairs to Go come from? Is the overhead high? Does the fair get a cut of the concessionaires' sales?"

"We have to pay the town a fee for the right to set up here, as well as rent on the site," Susan said. "The money goes to different town departments. As for taking a cut on what our concessionaires make, some shows do that, but we don't. The bookkeeping is too complicated. Besides, it gives people too much incentive to cheat."

"Then how—" Joe said.

Susan held up a hand. "Number one, admissions.

The town gets a small percentage, but the rest comes straight to us. Two, our concessionaires pay us a fee every month. The more people we manage to draw to the fairground, the higher the fee the concessionaires pay. So we've got two big reasons to try to attract as many people as we can. That's why these so-called accidents are harmful. Here, look at this."

She produced a newspaper clipping. The headline read: Fun Time at Fairs to Go? Not This Time.

"This was in this morning's paper. Apparently the writer's little girl got a terrible rash after she had her face painted at our show last week," Susan explained. "Her doctor said there was some kind of irritant in the face paint. Thousands of people must have seen this column. If the public starts thinking that Fairs to Go is unsafe, they'll stop coming. And what about the officials who decide which outfit to invite next year? Even a little thing can sway them, and this kind of publicity is not a little thing."

"I see that. But why isn't the show making money?" Frank asked in puzzlement. "This is the third day we've been here, and you've had good crowds every day. Not as good as you might like, but big enough."

"That's true, but we have a lot of expenses we have to meet," Susan replied. "Payroll, taxes, supplies . . . the list goes on and on. And for some reason, by the time we've paid the bills, there's nothing left."

She paused to rub her eyes, then laughed bitterly. "I ought to say, *less* than nothing," she continued. "There must be something I'm doing wrong, but I can't for the life of me figure out what. Maybe Ricky's

100

right. Maybe I don't have what it takes to run a big operation like this. Or maybe I'm just too young for the job."

"I think you're doing a fine job," Frank said firmly. "But the kind of dirty-tricks campaign you've faced would cause trouble for anyone, no matter how old and experienced."

She looked unconvinced.

"What about your competitors?" Frank went on. "Which of them would be happiest to see Fairs to Go fail?"

Susan stared down at her hands. "I hate to think that any of them would be happy," she said slowly. "But I guess . . . We're already over eighty percent booked for next year. If we go under, those bookings will all be up for grabs by the other outfits. And even if we stay alive, but word gets around that we're in trouble, some of our bookings will pull out and shop around."

"Those are pretty solid motives," Joe observed.

"I guess so," Susan said. She picked up a pencil and began to twist it between her fingers.

Joe decided to try another tack. "I get the feeling that most of the people who work for the show have been with it a long time."

"That's right," Susan replied, her face lighting up a little. "We've got a good, loyal bunch. I love every one of them."

"Has anyone been hired recently from another show? Somebody who might still have some kind of connection with one of your rivals?" Joe asked.

Susan shook her head. "I don't know all the people who work for the concessions," she said. "As far as our own crew goes, the only one I can think of is Ricky's friend, Boomer Harris. He was with Ruppert and Hess Spectaculars before he joined us."

"Boomer, huh?" Frank asked. "Exactly what is Boomer's job with Fairs to Go?"

"The same as it was with R and H," she replied. "He runs the nightly fireworks show. I guess that's why he's called Boomer," she added.

Frank looked over at Joe and saw that he was thinking the same thing. Raoul *wasn't* the only suspect in the Tunnel of Love attack, then, or even the best suspect. Boomer, too, had access to fireworks. The case was coming together at last.

There was a tap at the office door, and Morris stuck his head in. "Oh, sorry, Susan," he said. "I didn't know you were busy."

"That's okay," Frank said, getting to his feet. "We were just finishing." To Susan, he added, "We'll do everything we can."

"Thank you," she said gratefully.

As Frank followed Joe out the door, he heard Morris say, "Have you thought about my offer, Susan?"

Frank touched Joe on the shoulder and motioned for him to wait.

"No, I—" Susan said. Her voice broke. "This show was my dad's dream," she continued after a pause. "He put his whole life into it. How can I destroy that now, when he's so sick?"

"I know," Morris said. "It's really tough. But you have to decide, and right away. I want to do whatever I can, but I can't hold the offer open much longer. If we miss the payroll and have to close, our reputation will be shot. Can you give me an answer by tomorrow?"

"Yes," Susan said wearily. "Yes, I will."

Frank touched Joe's shoulder again, and they walked away quietly. When they were out of earshot, Joe said, "Our deadline just got two days shorter."

"It looks that way," Frank replied. "But I think we just got closer to a solution, too. It's time for another talk with Althea. She's still our best hope of finding out exactly what Ricky is up to."

When the Ferris wheel operator saw them coming, she suddenly became very involved in counting tickets. Behind her, the wheel turned steadily. Frank and Joe came to a halt in front of her and waited. Finally she looked up.

"We need to talk," Frank said.

"I told you before—" Althea began, pushing her ponytail back over her shoulder.

"That was before," Joe said, interrupting her. "Do you want Fairs to Go to fold?"

"Of course not," she replied. "I've got a lot of years invested in this outfit."

"Then you'd better do something right now to protect your investment," Frank said. "Otherwise, it may go down the tubes in the next twenty-four hours."

"Twenty-four hours? Are you putting me on?"

Althea looked from Frank to Joe. "No, I can see that you aren't."

She paused briefly to sell tickets to a family, who then joined the short line waiting for the next ride.

"I don't see how it can be as bad as that," Althea continued. "Sure, my ticket sales are down, especially after that little problem the first night here. But I'm still making out okay."

"Maybe so, but FTG isn't," Frank told her. "The situation's very serious. But maybe it can still be saved—*if* we get the cooperation we need."

For an endless moment, Althea stared out across the fairground, lost in thought. Then she shook her head. "If things are as bad as you say, I don't see how you guys can possibly turn it around," she said. "And I don't see what I can do to help, either. I'm sorry."

"Look, will you at least tell us what Ricky wanted from you?" Frank asked quickly.

Althea hesitated again. Finally, she said, "Why not? He wanted money."

"In return for what?" Joe asked. "Did he threaten you in any way?"

"Oh, no, it wasn't like that," she replied. "At least, not exactly. He gave me this story about how Susan was obviously messing up and how the major was going to be forced to make Ricky general manager in her place. At that point, Ricky would be in a position to do big favors for the people who deserved them."

"Meaning, people who gave him money?" Frank remarked.

Althea nodded. "He didn't say that in so many words, but I got the message just the same. The idea was that once he took over, he was going to need a war chest to put the show back on its feet. So he was asking for donations, as he called it."

"What did you say?" Joe asked.

"I told him, very nicely, to go climb a tree." She smiled. "And when he said I might be sorry I didn't help out when I had the chance, I threatened to tell Raoul that he'd been bothering me."

Frank laughed, then said, "Thanks, Althea. You've been a real help."

"I hope so," she replied with a deeply worried look. "I don't want to see this show go under. I'd manage to survive, I guess, but this bunch is like a family to me. I'd hate to lose that."

As they walked away, Frank said, "Well, we're finally getting to the bottom of things. Ricky and his two goons sabotage the show to make Susan look bad, so he can take her place as manager. Meanwhile he's doing a little not-so-subtle extortion to finance his campaign of dirty tricks. A very neat package."

"It's time we had a serious heart-to-heart with our pal Ricky," Joe said grimly.

"Exactly what I was thinking," Frank replied. "Let's split up and look for him. Whoever catches up with him first persuades him to go back to Susan's office for an important meeting. Okay?"

"How persuasive can I be?" Joe asked, his blue eyes twinkling.

"Use your own best judgment on that one," Frank said, grinning. "I'm going to take a closer look around West Avenue. As far as I know, Ricky hasn't covered the booths over there yet. What about you?"

Joe looked thoughtful. "I'm going to check out a hunch. If that doesn't pan out, I'll just wander around and keep my eyes open. Let's meet back at the Ferris wheel in half an hour, okay? Good hunting."

"Same to you," Frank said, already heading toward the farthest row of booths.

Joe returned to the Ferris wheel. "Althea?" he asked. "Where do Boomer and Kenny live?"

"In a camper on the back lot," she replied. "It's brown and white, with Utah plates. You can't miss it. Just look for the bright green furry dice hanging from the rearview mirror."

Five minutes later, Joe was cautiously circling the brown-and-white camper, examining it from all sides. In addition to the furry dice Althea had mentioned, it featured a collection of bumper stickers that covered the entire rear end. Joe read a few of the bumpers, shook his head, and murmured to himself, "How stupid can you get?"

Joe went to the door and knocked, but there was no answer. He tried again and waited, then looked around to see if he was being watched. He wasn't.

Uninvited visits always pay off, Joe thought, bending over to take a closer look at the lock. It was only slightly more complicated than the ones on cheap diaries. He unfolded the screwdriver blade of his pocketknife, inserted it in the lock, and gave a hard twist to the left. There was a loud click, and the door swung open.

Joe entered, carefully closing the door behind him. He took a quick look around. On a rack next to the door hung a familiar-looking red baseball cap. Joe had last seen it on Kenny's head, while the guy was trying to flatten him with a bumper car.

A fast search of the tiny kitchen turned up nothing of interest. The same went for the area around the driver's seat—until Joe pulled out the dashboard ashtray. There were several cigarette butts jammed into it. Joe fished one out and examined it. It was the same brand as the one Frank had found the day before, near the stack of soft-drink barrels. Still, Joe had to admit that lots of people smoked that brand.

Joe moved toward the rear of the camper, stepping over little piles of dirty clothes on the floor. There were two unmade bunks, and the sheets looked as if they hadn't been changed in weeks. Joe hurried past them, then stopped in front of a small dressing table. It was fastened to the wall, and its mirror was surrounded by small light bulbs.

Joe pulled open the dresser's middle drawer. Inside was a glass jar. The label read: Clown White— Guaranteed Hypoallergenic. Behind it were tubes, jars, and sticks of makeup—everything anyone needed to turn himself into a clown. There was also a tube of adhesive used by actors to attach false beards, eyebrows, and mustaches.

Kenny and Boomer apparently had many talents, Joe thought grimly.

As Joe was rummaging through the drawer, he heard a faint noise from the front of the camper. Either Boomer or Kenny was coming home!

Joe straightened up and quickly went through his options. Should he claim that he'd walked into the wrong camper? Say he was looking for a clown to hire for a birthday party? Simply try to leave, and deal with any opposition as best he could? Or should he hide?

Just then, a terrible sight filled the mirror. Joe realized that a clown had sneaked up behind him, a clown whose mad grin was filled with menace, the same clown who had been at the Hardys' kitchen window two nights before. Joe started to turn, but not in time. The clown raised a bulging sock and swung it with crushing force at the side of Joe's head.

12 The Fifth Clown

"Test your strength and ring the bell!" the barker called as Frank hurried by.

"Maybe next time," Frank said. As he turned onto one of the narrow cross streets, the noise of the crowds faded, and the sounds of the brass band and the calliope music from the carousel grew louder. A breeze wafted by, carrying the scents of popcorn, hot dogs, and hot candy-covered apples.

Frank's stomach let out a loud protest. He followed his nose to the candy apple stand and bought one.

He had just finished his first sticky, juicy bite when someone grabbed him from behind, lifted him high in the air, and flung him toward the ground. Frank broke the force of the fall with his left arm and leg, then rolled quickly away to keep his attacker from following up. He finished in a low crouch, facing his opponent in an aikido defense stance.

It was Raoul. He should have guessed, Frank thought. The former strongman was bent low at the waist, with his arms outspread. He glared at Frank, let out a growl, and charged. Frank scooped up a heaping handful of dirt and flung it straight at his eyes. As Raoul bellowed with rage and clawed at his face, Frank backed quickly out of reach.

Suddenly Chet came running toward them, with Althea right behind him. She rushed up to Raoul, putting herself between him and Frank.

"Raoul!" she shouted, grabbing one of his ears. "Stop it! Just stop it right now! What got into you? You're acting like an animal!"

Raoul shook his head and wiped his eyes. "He was getting fresh with you," he told her, pointing at Frank. "Nobody gets fresh with you, not while I'm around. Nobody!"

"Honestly," Althea exclaimed. "Me and Frank? That's crazy. Where'd you get that idea, you big lunk?"

"He saw you go in the Tunnel of Love with him and told me about it," Raoul said. "Why'd you go in the Tunnel of Love with him if he wasn't getting fresh with you?"

"'He'? Who's 'he'?" Althea demanded.

Raoul pointed at Frank once more. "Him, right there. The guy who threw dirt in my eyes."

Althea stamped her foot. "No, no! Who *told* you about us?"

110

Raoul looked away and kicked at the ground with his shoe. "He said not to tell anybody," he muttered.

"You can tell me," Althea said. "Who was it? Ricky?"

"No, it was Boomer," Raoul admitted. "You won't tell him I said so, will you? He said if I told, he wouldn't let me do the fireworks with him anymore."

Frank felt a surge of triumph at this damaging piece of evidence against Boomer. He stepped forward, although he was careful to stay out of Raoul's reach, just in case. "I don't think Boomer's going to be running the fireworks show much longer," he said.

Raoul's eyes widened. "You mean I can do the fireworks myself? That's what Ricky said when I gave him my money, but I didn't know if he meant it. Boomer's a friend of his."

"Oh, Raoul," Althea said, taking his arm. "You mean you gave that worm Ricky your savings?"

The former strongman nodded. "I had to. I want to be somebody important again, not just a nobody with big muscles. Ricky said I could be an important part of the show."

Althea looked over at Frank. "We'll get his money back, won't we?"

"Count on it," Frank replied. "Those guys are really low."

"Come with me, Raoul," Althea said. "We have to talk."

After they'd gone, Chet glanced at Frank. "Whew, that was a close one," he said, wiping his brow.

"Too close," Frank replied, brushing himself off.

"But your timing was perfect. I was starting to wonder if I could manage to outrun that human steam shovel. How did you know?"

Chet looked offended. "I was supposed to follow him, remember?" he said. "So I did. I saw Boomer talking to him, but I wasn't close enough to hear what they were saying. It's too bad. If I had, maybe I could have warned you."

"That's okay," Frank said. "You couldn't have known what was going down."

Chet nodded. "That's true. Anyway, when I followed Raoul here and saw him start to attack you, I ran to get Althea. I would have tried to come to your rescue myself, but that would have just gotten us both torn to bits."

"Good thinking," Frank said, clapping his friend on the back. "You did just the right thing. Now, I think you'd better get back on Raoul's tail, just in case Kenny or Boomer tries to turn him on us again. I'm going after the ringleader, Ricky."

After leaving Chet, Frank continued on to West Avenue, but Ricky wasn't there. Frowning, he decided to make his way back across the fairground.

When he passed the shooting gallery, he spotted Farkas leaning on the counter, looking very sour. When the barker noticed Frank, his expression became even more sour.

On impulse, Frank went over to him. "Not much business today," he remarked.

"What's it to you?" Farkas replied, glaring at Frank.

"Nothing," Frank said. Then it occurred to him to try a bluff. "But I thought you should know—the bribe you gave Ricky is money down the drain. It isn't going to buy you anything."

Farkas straightened up. He tried to look uninterested, but Frank could see the alarm in his eyes.

"Your jaw's wagging, but nothing's coming out that makes sense," Farkas snarled.

Frank rolled his eyes. "Come off it, buddy," he said. "Ricky told you you could stay on if you helped him take over the management of the show. 'Helped' meant give him money."

He pointed his forefinger at Farkas and continued, "So you did it. But you never stopped to think what would happen when Susan found out. Which she is going to, when I see her in about fifteen minutes. You can forget about your two weeks' notice, Farkas. You'll be lucky if she lets you stay open the rest of the evening."

Farkas's Adam's apple bobbed up and down as he swallowed convulsively. He cleared his throat and said, "You got it wrong, pal. I didn't give Ricky any bribes."

Frank gave him a look full of cold menace. "Don't lie to me, Farkas," he said.

The shooting gallery operator took a step backward. "I'm not lying," he protested. "Okay, okay, I gave Ricky some money, but it wasn't a bribe. It was a . . . a commission. Yeah, that's it, a commission. He said he'd help me place my operation, shift it to a spot in the show that had more traffic. That way, I'd draw more customers, right? So I gave him an advance on his commission, that's all. Just normal business."

Farkas glanced both ways and lowered his voice. "I'm a firm believer in helping people who help me, you know what I mean? Take you. You seem to have a lot of pull with Susan, am I right? Now, if you were to use your influence to get her to forget this dumb idea of throwing me out of the show, I wouldn't forget it. I'm a firm believer in gratitude. You see my point?"

Frank's mouth curled in disgust. "I see your point, all right," he replied. "If you want some free advice, you'd better start packing. You're finished with Fairs to Go."

Frank walked away before Farkas could reply. He had just gathered another piece of evidence against Ricky. That was certainly worth the trouble of dealing with that lowlife Farkas, he told himself. The outlines of Ricky's extortion scheme were becoming clearer with every witness he spoke to.

As Frank neared the Ski-Bob, he saw Raoul walking in his direction. Frank took a deep breath, clenched his fists, and dug his heel into the ground, ready to face the ex-strongman. But apparently, Althea's lecture had gotten through to him. He gave Frank a look that was a little short on friendliness, but that was all.

A moment later, Chet strolled by, seemingly aimless, but clearly on Raoul's tail. As he passed Frank, he lifted a king-size box of popcorn in salute, then frowned as some of the popcorn spilled out onto the ground. Amused, Frank watched as Chet shrugged and moved on.

The four Fratellis were performing in the center of the midway. Over the heads of the crowd, Frank saw that all of the clowns had instruments this time—accordion, clarinet, guitar, and snare drum. They belted out a tune with an Afro-Cuban beat, while stilt-dancing, spinning, and kicking high in the air.

The rhythm was contagious. A lot of the fair-goers were dancing, and even those who weren't swayed in place. Frank exchanged smiles with a young woman who was carrying a two-year-old on her shoulders, then walked on with a new bounce in his stride.

After another five minutes of searching, Frank stopped near the Fun House. So far, Ricky hadn't turned up. Had he left the fairground? Maybe whoever was taking tickets at the front gate had noticed him go. It was worth a try.

As he turned to make his way to the front gate, Frank glanced to his left, down the narrow gap between the Fun House and a booth that printed people's photos on T-shirts. At that moment, he saw one of the Fratellis, in costume but no longer on stilts, racing by the gap on the other side.

Frank walked on a few steps, listening to the distant Afro-Cuban music. Suddenly, he stopped in his tracks. The clown he had just caught a glimpse of *looked* like one of the Fratellis. But why hadn't he been on stilts and holding an instrument? And who was playing the music in the distance, if not the four clowns?

But if the clown he had just seen wasn't one of the Fratellis, who was he?

13 A Secret Meeting

Frank turned and ran back to the gap between the Fun House and the T-shirt booth, then into the alley behind them. But the clown was gone. Frank ran about twenty yards down the alley, glancing into the spaces between various booths as he went, but it was no use.

Frowning, he turned and retraced his steps to the place where he had seen the Fratellis performing a few minutes earlier, wondering if the mysterious clown might be the same one who had set the booby trap at his house.

The Fratellis were still there, all four of them, surrounded by the same cheering crowd.

Of course, Frank thought. At a carnival, a clown costume and makeup was the perfect disguise. You

117

could do your dirty work without anyone paying attention to you. And even if someone did notice you, he or she wouldn't be able to identify you later. The only drawback was that you would have to be careful to stay out of the way of the real clowns. *They* would certainly notice you if you crossed their path.

As Frank circled behind the crowd, he noticed Susan up ahead and joined her.

"Aren't they great?" she said, gesturing toward the Fratellis. Frank heard a note of sadness in her voice. "I love everything about the show, but I've always had a special soft spot for the clowns. Whenever I'm feeling blue, I just watch them for a little while and I feel better." She added ruefully, "But it doesn't seem to be working this time."

"Are there any other clowns with Fairs to Go?" Frank asked. "Or are they it?"

Susan looked at him in surprise. "With the four Fratellis in the show, who could possibly need anyone else?" she asked defensively. "Why?"

"I thought I saw someone else in a clown costume a little while ago," Frank replied.

"It's funny you should say that," Susan said, frowning. "About twenty minutes ago, on my way over here, I thought I saw a clown I didn't know. But I was too far away to be sure. What does it mean, Frank?" She sighed. "More trouble of some kind, I'm sure. That's about all we seem to have these days—trouble."

"Yes, well . . . let's go somewhere we can talk quietly," Frank said.

"Sure." Susan led him to the crew's mess tent on

118

the back lot. The place was empty. As they sat down at a table, Susan said, "More bad news?"

"I'm afraid so," Frank replied. "Look, I don't want to upset you, but you'd better know the truth. Ricky has been going around to all the concessionaires, demanding money and promising them special treatment once he takes over the show. Apparently, a lot of them have been going along with him."

Susan dropped her eyes. "I . . . I'm not really surprised," she said in a tired voice. "Upset, yes, but not surprised. I wasn't going to tell you this, but not long after my father's heart attack, we discovered some money missing from the safe. Aside from Morris and me, Ricky was the only one who knew the combination. He finally admitted 'borrowing' it and paid it back, but I haven't trusted him ever since."

"What did your father say when he found out?" Frank asked.

Susan shook her head. "We never told him. He was in no shape to learn that his stepson was a thief. I know that's a harsh word, but it's the only one that fits. So we hushed it up."

" 'We'?" Frank asked.

"Morris and I are the only ones who know about it. And now you."

"Susan?" Frank began. "You said earlier that you couldn't figure out why Fairs to Go isn't making a profit. Is there some way that Ricky could be diverting some of the money, siphoning it off into his own pocket?"

"I don't know," she replied slowly. "Morris keeps a

pretty close watch on the financial side of things. I wouldn't think that Ricky could put anything over on him. But maybe he learned some tricks in business school that Morris and I don't know about."

Susan was silent for a moment. "How could he do such a thing!" she burst out finally. "He's been making promises about what he'll do when he takes over the show, has he? Well, unless the situation changes fast, there won't be any show for him to take over!"

"Joe and I have been looking for Ricky," Frank said. "Have you seen him?"

"No, I haven't. He's been avoiding me the past couple of days. Now I understand why," she said bitterly.

"I'm going to find him," Frank said. "We'll make him give back any money he's taken and see to it that Fairs to Go survives."

Susan put her hand over his. "I know you will," she said softly. "And I don't have to tell you how grateful I am—how grateful everyone in the show will be—to you and your brother. You two, and your friend Chet, are the only bright spots in this whole mess."

Frank stood up, feeling slightly embarrassed. "I'd better keep looking for Ricky. Now more than ever, it's important that I find him—fast."

After saying goodbye, Frank headed for the main entrance to the fairground. The guy taking tickets looked familiar, but Frank didn't know his name, so he introduced himself.

120

"Hi, Frank, I'm Pete Carroll," the man replied, offering his hand. "What can I do for you?"

"Susan needs to talk to Ricky. You haven't seen him leaving the fairground, have you?" Frank asked.

"Ricky?" Pete thought for a moment, then shook his head. "Nope, I haven't seen him all day."

"How long have you been at the gate?"

"I came on at two," Pete replied. "He might have left before then. Or he might have gone out without me noticing. I mostly pay attention to the people coming in, not the ones leaving."

Pete paused to take some tickets from a family of five. He tore them in half and handed the stubs to the mother, then clicked the counter on his belt. "Have fun at the fair," he told them.

Pete turned back to Frank. "Anything else I can do for you?"

"No, that's it. Thanks, Pete," Frank replied.

"If I see Ricky," Pete volunteered, "I'll tell him you're looking for him."

"Don't bother," Frank said. "I'll find him."

Frank turned back down the midway. The late afternoon crowd was bigger than ever, and most of the people had happy expressions on their faces. There were long lines waiting for the Phantom Jet, the Mad Mouse, and the Giant Whip. There was even a group watching a man demonstrate a wire gadget that was supposed to make any closet hold three times as much.

Everywhere Frank looked, people were eating

delicious-looking sausage sandwiches, slices of pizza, and shish kebabs. His stomach reminded him that all he had eaten in the last few hours was a single bite of a candy apple.

He stopped at the pizza stand and asked for a slice. While he waited for it, deep in thought, he watched the crowd flow by. Even if the fair wasn't doing as well as last year, it was obviously attracting a lot of people, Frank mused. And all of them bought admission tickets. So how could the operation be losing so much money?

Frank took his slice and went back to the entrance gate. He waited while Pete took care of a small bunch of fair-goers, then said, "I'm confused about how admissions are handled. People buy their tickets over there at the booth, then give them to you, right?"

"Sure," Pete replied. "Then I tear them in half and give them the stubs."

"What's to stop someone from giving you a phony ticket?" Frank continued.

Pete fished one of the ticket halves from the box in front of him and offered it to Frank. "Look," he said. "It says Fairs to Go in big letters, and there's a serial number on both halves of the ticket. Besides, anyone trying that would have to know an awful lot about our operation. The color of the ticket changes every day. We don't even know what it'll be until just before we open."

"I see," Frank said. "But what if the person selling the tickets had his own supply of tickets in different

122

colors? Couldn't he sell people those, and keep the money for himself?"

Pete's face reddened. "Listen," he said tightly. "I won't swear that things like that never happen. But not when *I'm* on the gate."

He patted the counter on his belt. "You see this? When I go off duty, I record how many people I've let in on the summary sheet. And it had better be pretty close to the number of tickets the guy in the booth sold during my shift, or someone is in very big trouble."

Frank nodded. "I see," he said. He stared at the ground thoughtfully. "In other words, the only way a scheme like that could work is if the ticket seller and the ticket taker were in on it together," he murmured to himself.

"Would you care to spell out what you're getting at, Frank?" Pete asked, his voice rippling with tension. "Or would you like a knuckle sandwich for dinner?"

Frank glanced up, surprised. Pete was facing him with clenched fists.

"Hey, I'm sorry," Frank said, holding his hands up. "I didn't mean anything, I was just talking to myself."

"I've been six years with Fairs to Go, and no one ever had a word to say against me," Pete continued, still clearly angry.

Frank wished that he'd been more careful in his choice of words. "Listen, Pete," he said, "all I meant was that the system sounds pretty foolproof. I wasn't accusing you of anything, really."

Pete glared at him for another moment, then turned away. "Well, okay," he said. "But the next time you get thoughts like that, you keep them to yourself, you hear? Otherwise, people might get the wrong idea."

"I'll do that, thanks," Frank said. But Pete ignored him.

Frank shrugged and walked back toward the midway. He had a feeling that he had just learned something very important, but he wasn't sure what. If Pete had been telling the truth, the system in place made it very hard to skim money from ticket sales. Yet it was pretty clear that someone was diverting money somewhere, somehow. Ricky was the strongest suspect as far as motive went, but what about means and opportunity? Susan had said she and Morris kept Ricky away from the office as much as possible. Maybe this case wasn't as close to a solution as he and Joe had thought a couple of hours earlier.

He glanced at his watch. Time to meet Joe at the Ferris wheel.

But when Frank got there, Joe was nowhere to be seen. Frank frowned. If Joe had cornered Ricky, maybe things had gotten rough. . . .

Just then, Frank heard angry voices. A couple with two kids was standing in front of the cotton candy booth, arguing with the woman behind the counter. The father was waving a partly eaten puff of cotton candy in each hand, and the two kids looked ready to burst into tears.

"Just taste one of these!" the father shouted at the

woman. "You think I'm going to let you poison my kids?"

"No one has ever complained before," the woman said, raising her voice. "You can't expect to get your money back, just because your children changed their minds."

"Changed their minds? They nearly got sick after one bite. We had to give up our place in the line for the pony ride!" the father told her huffily.

"That's not my fault," the woman retorted.

Frank hurried over and took out his wallet. "Excuse me," he said. "I'm with Fairs to Go. How much were the two cotton candies?"

The father told him, and Frank handed him the correct amount. "I'm sorry there was a problem," Frank said. "I hope you enjoy the rest of your visit to the fair. Oh—may I have the two cotton candies?"

"You're welcome to them," the father said, thrusting them into Frank's hands. "Come on, kids, let's get back on line for the ponies."

The woman behind the counter gave Frank a suspicious look. "What is this?" she said. "I don't know you."

"I'm new," he said, showing her his pass from Susan. Then he took a little piece of cotton candy and put it in his mouth.

"Ugh," he said, and spat it out. The sugar was completely overwhelmed by the taste of salt.

"What is it?" the woman said. She was beginning to look alarmed.

Frank handed her some of the cotton candy. She tasted it and made a face. "I don't understand," she said. "I haven't had any complaints until just now."

She dipped her finger into the drum that spun the cotton candy, then put a bit of the bright pink mixture into her mouth. "Yuck!" she cried out. "It's pure salt. There must have been salt in my bag of sugar. But how did it get there?"

"Did you just open a new bag?" Frank asked. "Maybe there was a mistake at the factory."

She shook her head. "I've been using sugar from that bag all day. I don't understand it."

Frank studied the booth. The big paper bag of sugar was right underneath the counter. Anyone could reach over and pour something into it—if no one was watching.

"Have you been here the whole time?" he asked.

"Sure," the woman replied. "Well—not the *whole* time. I took a break about an hour ago. But somebody covered for me. I can't afford to shut down as long as there are customers around, you know."

"And when did you make this batch of cotton candy—before your break, or after it?"

"I just made it five minutes ago," she said. "Why?"

"Is this the first batch you made since your break?" Frank continued.

"Well, sure. I make a new batch every hour, hour and a half, depending on the traffic. Say, what is all this?" she added warily.

"Look, I'm trying to help you," Frank replied,

annoyed. He had had about as much as he could take of the carnival people's suspiciousness. "Who watched the stand while you were away?"

"Why, Kenny did," she replied. "It was really nice of him to offer, too."

Frank nodded. "Thanks," he said. "And if I were you, I'd throw out that batch of cotton candy and what's left in that sugar bag. You don't want anyone to get sick and sue you."

Her jaw dropped. Frank didn't wait for her response. He had a job to do.

Kenny, he thought as he walked away. It figured. One more dirty trick to put on the account of Ricky and his friends. But where *was* Ricky, and where was Joe?

Frank was just passing the big plastic bubble of the Moonwalk when he spotted Kenny down a narrow lane to his right. The guy was standing almost out of sight, smoking a cigarette and talking to someone whose back was to Frank. Dodging behind a stack of crates, Frank tried to listen, but their voices were so low that he couldn't hear.

Frank sighed in frustration. Talk louder, he ordered them silently. Then, as if in answer, Kenny raised his voice.

"Okay, I'll do it," he said. "But it's gonna cost you. If I take a chance like this, I expect it to pay off big."

Frank peered from behind the crates, then ducked back. Kenny was walking quickly in Frank's direction. Frank was sure he'd be spotted. But Kenny paused

127

just long enough to throw his cigarette on the ground and stamp on it, then strode past Frank's hiding place without a single glance.

Frank risked another look. He *had* to know who Kenny's companion was.

The other person turned and stepped out of the shadow. Frank stared, unbelieving. It was Morris Tuttle.

14 Fire!

Frank shrank back into the shelter of the crates, his mind racing. What was Morris doing talking to Kenny? Was Morris in cahoots with Ricky, too? But that didn't make sense—did it?

As Morris walked past his hiding place, Frank kept still as a stone. But the beginnings of an idea were forming in his mind.

He let Morris get several yards away before silently moving out from behind the crates. He started walking, taking care to make plenty of noise. Morris spun around.

"Frank!" he exclaimed. "You gave me quite a scare. You never know who might be lurking in these dark alleys."

Frank smiled. "Sorry," he said. "Hey, who was that

I saw you with just now? It looked a lot like that hood, Kenny." He watched Morris closely as he spoke.

The business manager's smile faded. "Yes, it was Kenny," he admitted. "And I have to say, Frank, I'm sorry."

"Sorry for what?" Frank was a little confused. Where was Morris trying to lead him?

"You were right about the sabotage all along!" Morris said, sounding angry. "I should have listened to you earlier. I just found out that Ricky Delgado actually hired Kenny and that thug, Boomer, to ruin FTG. So I explained to Kenny that unless he agrees to testify against Ricky, he'll end up in jail right alongside him."

Frank didn't know what to believe. Either Morris was a very quick thinker, or he was telling the truth. What he was saying sounded reasonable enough. . . .

Morris clapped Frank on the shoulder. "I think this case is at an end, my friend. You and your brother can stop worrying about it."

"Great," Frank managed to say. "I'm sure Joe will be glad it's wrapped up. And I can't wait to tell Susan. Look, I've got to run—I'm late to meet Joe now."

He hurried off toward the Ferris wheel, his thoughts churning. Morris should have stopped talking while he was ahead, he thought. If he hadn't sounded so eager to get rid of the Hardys, Frank might have bought his story. But now . . . Frank shook his head. Morris was involved—but how, exactly? The case was still unclear in his mind. He needed to talk it over with Joe.

At the Ferris wheel, there was still no sign of Joe. Frank looked at his watch, and anxiety began to make his scalp prickle. Joe was nearly twenty minutes late. Where was he?

Frank went up to Althea's ticket booth. "Excuse me," he said. "Has my brother been by here recently?"

"Sorry," she replied. "I haven't seen him in the last couple of hours." Then she took a closer look at Frank's face. "Is something wrong?"

"I hope not," Frank muttered. He was beginning to get a bad feeling in his gut.

"The last time I saw him, he was asking where Boomer and Kenny live," Althea said. She described their camper. "Does that help?"

"Maybe it does," Frank said grimly. "Thanks!"

He ran across the fairground to the trailer park and soon tracked down the brown-and-white camper. He banged on the door, but there was no answer.

Frank tried the doorknob. It was unlocked. He stepped cautiously inside and looked around. No one was there.

Near the back, he found a lighted dressing table. Beside it a chair lay on its side. On a hunch, he opened a drawer in the dressing table.

"Clown white," he muttered. "And other makeup, too. That adds up to a fake clown—like the one in our backyard. And that chair didn't fall over by itself, either. There was a fight here."

Frank's jaw tensed. He was certain now that Joe was in serious trouble. But where was he?

131

Frank left the camper, returned to the fairground, and began combing it. As he went down one line of booths and up the next, he asked everyone for news of Joe. But no one had any to give him.

As he was passing the carousel for what seemed like the seventeenth time, Frank saw Carl up ahead. He pushed through the crowd and caught up to him.

"Joe?" Carl said, when Frank posed his question. "Let me think . . . the last time I saw him was two or three hours ago. He and Farkas got into a fight, and I had to sort it out. Is that any help?"

Frank shook his head. "No, I've seen him myself since then. How about Boomer or Kenny or Ricky? Have you seen any of them lately?"

"Boomer and Kenny, no," Carl replied. "But I saw Ricky just a few minutes ago. He was going into the House of Mirrors with one of the clowns."

"You mean one of the four Fratelli Brothers?" Frank demanded.

Carl frowned. "That's a funny thing," he said. "Now that you ask, I'm not absolutely sure it was one of the Fratellis. But it had to be. They're the only clowns we've got in the show."

"The only *real* clowns," Frank said grimly. He pointed to the left. "The House of Mirrors is over that way, isn't it?"

"That's right," Carl said. "Go to the end of this row, then it's two rows over."

Frank set off quickly, dodging through the crowd. After a few steps, he broke into a run. He couldn't think of any legitimate reason for Ricky and one of his henchmen—dressed as a clown—to be visiting the House of Mirrors. And it was hard to imagine a better place to conceal a captive.

At the House of Mirrors, Frank showed his pass to the woman at the entrance. "Is Ricky Delgado still inside?" he asked her.

"I haven't seen him leave yet," she replied. "Say, I don't know you, do I?"

"No, I'm new," Frank said.

"Oh. Okay, have fun. If you get lost, just follow the dots on the ceiling—they'll lead you to the exit."

"Thanks," Frank said, and hurried through the entrance. Three steps inside, he bumped into what turned out to be a pane of clear glass.

"This is trickier than I thought," he told himself. He glanced up at the ceiling. There was an inconspicuous dot of white paint on the right side of the mirrored corridor. But there was another mirror there . . . wasn't there? Frank put out a tentative hand. It passed right through the place he expected a mirror to be. Someone had put a lot of cleverness into the design of this maze, he thought.

A girl in jeans and an "Earth—Love It or Leave It" T-shirt walked straight into Frank and gasped with surprise. "You're real!" she said.

"I hope so," Frank replied.

"I'm sorry, I thought you were another of those mirror images," the girl continued, laughing. "I can't tell the difference anymore."

133

Frank suddenly stiffened. He turned his head to one side, then the other, sniffing the air. "I smell smoke," he said.

A look of alarm crossed the girl's face. "So do I," she said. "It's getting stronger, too."

Somewhere nearby, a man yelled, "Fire!" Two or three others started screaming. Then there was a loud thud as a panicky fair-goer crashed into the other side of the mirror on Frank's left.

Frank realized that the situation was quickly becoming a disaster. He cupped his hands around his mouth, took a deep breath, and shouted, *"Listen, everybody!* Follow my directions, and we'll all be all right!"

Silence fell. "Get down on your hands and knees, below the level of the smoke, and move quietly toward the exit," Frank continued. "There are dots on the ceiling that mark the way. Stay calm, and everyone will get out safely."

People got on their hands and knees and began crawling along. Frank pressed himself against a mirror to let a family of four get by. They were all wide-eyed with terror, and the youngest, a boy of about six, looked as though he was about to faint.

The girl who had bumped into Frank dropped to her knees and said, "We'd better get moving."

She was right. The smoke, grayish white and smelling of chemicals, was already filling the upper part of the corridor. Frank's throat felt raw from it.

"This way!" Frank shouted over his shoulder. A

134

small crowd of people crawled after him. Suddenly a man in jeans and a knit shirt jumped to his feet and started screaming. "We're all going to die! We're going to be burned to death!"

The man next to him leapt up and socked him in the jaw, then began dragging him after the others.

"Attention, attention," a voice boomed from up ahead. "Please follow my voice and stay calm. You will not be in any danger if you stay calm and follow directions. Help is on the way."

Frank gave a sigh of relief. But what about Ricky and his thug . . . and Joe?"

"You go ahead, back that way," Frank told the girl. "I've got something I have to do first."

She gave him a dubious look, as if she wanted to argue, but then was overwhelmed by a coughing fit. That decided her. "Okay, but you'd better make it fast," she said, and began crawling back down the corridor. The small crowd followed after her.

Bent over double, Frank started in the other direction. He hadn't gone more than a few feet when someone in a clown costume and makeup appeared out of nowhere, shouldered him out of the way, and raced off toward the exit. Fearing the worst, Frank quickly turned in the direction the clown had come from and started trying to penetrate the maze. Smoke stung his eyes, sweat was pouring down his face, and each breath was more painful than the last. But he pushed on.

And then, from behind one of the mirrors, Frank

135

heard a cough. He cocked his head and listened. Again, there was a weak cough. Someone was trapped behind the mirror!

He rapped on the glass and shouted, "Is anybody there?"

This time, he heard a faint groan.

Without hesitating, Frank covered his face with his elbow and kicked the mirror as hard as he could. The mirror exploded like a bomb. Glass flew in all directions.

Frank peered through the thickening smoke. Ricky was lying facedown on the floor, barely conscious. Shards of glass from the broken mirror glittered on his back. Just beyond him, bound and gagged but conscious and alert, was Joe.

As Frank rushed over to his brother, he heard an ominous crackling sound from his right. He glanced over quickly. The mirrored wall on that side had shattered. Lurid orange flames were endlessly reflected in the other mirrored walls of the maze. The countless reflections made it impossible to judge exactly how close the flames were, but Frank could feel their heat searing his face and bare arms. How could he possibly untie his brother, rouse Ricky, and get them all to safety in time? In another moment, it would be too late for the three of them to escape a horrible death.

15 Time for Some Fun

Frank decided to start with Joe's gag.

"My knife," Joe gasped when Frank had removed the gag. "Right pants pocket."

Frank found the knife and opened it to the sharpest blade. As he sawed desperately at the ropes around Joe's wrists and ankles, he asked, "Do you think you can move?"

"I think so," Joe replied. "Let's get out of here— fast!"

Frank gestured toward Ricky. "We'll have to drag him."

The smoke was too thick to even think of standing up. Frank rolled Ricky over onto his back, then grabbed him under the left armpit. Joe got behind him and pushed.

137

After a few seconds, Frank gasped, "This isn't going to work. Can you lift him onto my back?"

"I'll try," Joe responded. Together, they wrestled Ricky's limp body onto Frank's back. It seemed to take an eternity. Finally they were able to start crawling toward the exit again. Frank did his best to avoid the broken glass on the floor, but a sharp pain in his right knee told him that he hadn't quite succeeded.

Suddenly, Frank bumped into a mirror. The corridor he thought he had seen was actually a dead end! A *real* dead end, for all three of them, he thought grimly. Then he remembered the dots. He craned his neck and stared upward, but the smoke was too thick for him to see the ceiling from the floor.

There was only one thing to do. Taking a deep breath, he let Ricky roll off his back, then sprang to his feet and peered upward. He fell back to his knees with tears streaming down his cheeks.

"Left," he gasped to Joe, and maneuvered Ricky onto his back again. Ricky seemed much heavier. Then Frank realized what was going on. Ricky wasn't heavier, *he* was weakening, and so was Joe. Would their strength hold out long enough to escape the flaming maze? As if in answer, his elbows gave way and he fell, facedown, to the floor.

"Come on, Frank," Joe panted. "We can do it. It's just a little way, now. I'll take Ricky."

"No, it's okay," Frank mumbled in reply. He counted to three and pushed himself up onto his hands and knees. But how much longer could he last?

138

The smoke was filling the narrow maze from ceiling to floor, and the heat of the flames felt as if they were only a few feet behind the three guys.

Then Frank felt a cool breeze on his cheek. Was he becoming delirious, or . . .

"Joe, come on!" Frank tried to shout. What came out was a raspy whisper. "This way! We're safe!"

Suddenly, Ricky's weight was lifted from his back. Frank looked up and saw a space monster looming over him.

It was a fire fighter wearing a respirator mask. Another fire fighter rushed past Frank and into the maze. Frank and Joe crawled the last few feet out of the fire-ravaged House of Mirrors and into the late afternoon sunlight. Sprawled on his back, Frank gulped in a lungful of fresh air and started coughing helplessly.

He finally managed to sit up. Joe was on the ground next to him, propped up on one elbow, and just beyond him was Ricky, gazing around with a dazed look on his face.

Susan and Morris came rushing over.

"Joe! Frank!" Susan exclaimed. "Thank goodness you're safe. I was so worried."

"What about me?" Ricky demanded sullenly. "Don't I count?"

"You," Morris snarled. "You can start counting the years you'll spend in jail!"

"Jail?" Ricky said, rubbing his eyes. "What are you talking about?"

"I'm talking about theft, arson, racketeering, at-

139

tempted murder . . . and that's just for starters," Morris replied. "The police are on their way here now. I called them myself."

"That's crazy!" Ricky proclaimed, struggling to sit up. "I didn't do anything!"

Frank struggled to his feet. "What were you doing in the House of Mirrors?" he asked Ricky.

Ricky looked confused. "I don't know . . . oh, yeah. I passed this clown who looked like one of the Fratellis, but then I realized that he wasn't. Then it came to me. He had to be one of the people trying to wreck the show."

Ricky gave Susan a sidelong look. "I figured if I could solve the case while Susan's pet detectives were making fools of themselves, the major would *have* to put me in charge of FTG. So I followed the clown into the House of Mirrors. The next thing I knew, I was waking up out here, with the mother of all headaches."

"Joe?" Frank asked. "How about you? What do you remember?"

"All I know," Joe replied, "is that a clown knocked me out. When I came to, I was tied up and lying in the mirror maze. A few minutes later, the clown dragged Ricky in, dumped him on the floor, and ran out. Then I smelled smoke. You know the rest."

Frank rubbed the soot on his cheek. "I've got to wash this stuff off," he announced. "What about you, Joe?" He gave his brother a significant look, and Joe nodded.

The brothers walked around a corner, out of sight of the others. "What's going on?" Joe demanded quietly. "The clown who slugged me had to be either Boomer or Kenny. I got caught searching their camper. But why would he knock Ricky out and leave him in the House of Mirrors if Ricky's his boss? It doesn't make sense."

"I have an idea about that," Frank declared. "Ricky's no innocent little lamb, but he's *not* the one masterminding the sabotage."

"Then who is? Farkas?" Joe suggested tentatively.

Frank shook his head. "A little while ago, I saw Kenny talking to Morris Tuttle. He said something about how Morris was going to have to pay big money for something he was about to do. Afterward, Morris told me that Ricky is behind the sabotage and that he'd convinced Kenny to turn on him. But I think Morris was lying to me."

"You mean Kenny is really working for Morris!" Joe said excitedly. "So that's why the fair is losing money —the business manager is a crook!"

"Come on," Frank said. He turned and walked quickly in the direction of the trailer park.

Joe hurried after him. "Where are we going?" he asked breathlessly. "Can you give me a hint?"

"Sure," Frank replied as they approached the office trailer. "It just occurred to me. What kind of responsible business manager keeps all the firm's records only on a hard drive? That's just asking to lose them."

141

Frank tried the door. It was unlocked. He led Joe through Susan's office to Morris's cubicle. "Start searching, Joe," he said. "We're looking for floppy disks—*any* floppy disks."

Joe began looking through the file cabinet, while Frank sat down and started working on the lock to the desk.

"Nothing here," Joe reported, just as Frank managed to get the desk open.

Frank began looking through the drawers. Nothing but stationery in the first drawer, he noted, and the second held only pencils, paper clips, rubber bands, and the kind of junk that seemed to grow in desk drawers. The center drawer wasn't tall enough for a box of diskettes, but he checked it anyway.

"Nothing here, either," Frank told Joe with frustration in his voice. "It doesn't make sense. Anyone who uses a computer on a daily basis has to have diskettes around."

Frank started to check the desk drawers once more. Then something struck him as odd. The second drawer seemed to be shorter than the first, by about three inches. While Joe watched, Frank pulled it out all the way, raised the front of it slightly to lift the rollers past the stops, then pulled again. Behind the back wall was a narrow compartment, and in it were two diskette boxes.

Frank picked up one of them. It was labeled FTG Accounts Back-up. He turned to show it to Joe, but at that moment, someone grabbed his shoulders and forced him backward in the chair, while a hand

142

reached out and seized the box of diskettes. Some-where behind him, Joe grunted in pain.

Frank's well-honed martial arts instincts took over. He bent his knees, braced his feet against the edge of the desk, and thrust his body and the desk chair back with all his force. He felt the chair slam into his attacker's stomach.

"Oof!" Frank's attacker released his shoulders.

Frank threw himself sideways, out of the chair, and rolled to his feet. He saw that his attacker was Kenny, who was now doubled over on the floor, clutching his stomach. Frank also saw that Joe was grappling with someone in clown costume. Joe had just gotten an arm lock on the clown—obviously Boomer—who was crying out, "Okay, okay, I give up!"

The battle was over in less than a minute. But where was the box of diskettes?

As if in answer, the trailer door slammed shut.

"Morris!" Frank shouted to Joe. "He's got the evidence. Stay here with these guys—I'll catch him."

Frank dashed out of the trailer and looked both ways. Morris was just turning onto the midway.

The fleeing business manager had a big lead. Frank sprinted after him, but the dense crowds slowed him down. He sidestepped around a woman pushing a toddler in a stroller, only to crash into a heavyset guy in a University of Nevada sweatshirt. The guy tried to grab him, but Frank slithered out of his grasp and kept running. A painful stitch in his side reminded Frank that he still hadn't recovered from inhaling all that smoke.

He managed to close the gap to fifteen or twenty yards, but it still seemed possible that Morris would reach the parking lot with enough of a lead to escape.

As he was passing the shooting gallery, Frank looked ahead and saw Chet. He was just stepping away from one of the food concessions with a big slice of pizza in his hand.

"Chet!" Frank shouted. "Stop him!"

Startled, Chet looked up just as Morris was passing him. Chet instantly flung his slice of pizza straight at Morris's head. Temporarily blinded by the hot, melted mozzarella, the crooked manager collided with a fair-goer, tripped, and fell to the ground. Before he could get back on his feet, Frank was standing over him.

"Thanks for calling the police," Frank said to Morris as the sound of sirens drew closer. "You saved us the trouble."

The next afternoon Joe, Frank, Chet, and Susan met at the fairground. Joe had just returned from Con Riley's office, where he had heard the latest on the case.

"What's your pleasure?" a bright-eyed Susan asked. "Today this place belongs to you guys."

"How about the Space Capsule?" Chet suggested.

Susan said, "You got it."

They walked over to East Avenue and filed aboard the capsule. The circular bench inside was just big enough for the four of them. As the capsule began to rise and spin gently, Susan said, "So it was Morris all along. But he and Dad were partners for years. Why would he want to destroy his own business?"

"I can guess," Frank said. The capsule was now beginning to rotate as well as spin. "You've been drawing good crowds, but losing money, right? It doesn't add up—unless a lot of the money the show should be getting is going somewhere else."

"But we have really good controls over the box office," Susan protested.

Joe nodded. "We know. That should have been the tip-off. If the money wasn't being skimmed up front, it had to be going out at the wrong places—and only the show's business manager was in a position to arrange that."

Frank took up the story. "You'll find that Fairs to Go has been paying for a lot of goods and services it never received to companies that exist only in Morris's imagination. And it's probably been going on for months, maybe years."

"Tuttle's admitted to the cops that he's been embezzling from the firm," Joe reported. "He didn't have much choice. Those computer disks we found are loaded with evidence of his crooked scheme."

"It makes me sick to think that Morris was stealing from the show," Susan said. "But I still don't understand why he tried to wreck it."

Frank gazed at the twisting, twirling landscape outside the capsule. "Morris has probably been stealing from the show for years, as I said. But when your father had his heart attack, Morris suddenly realized that he was in terrible danger. If your father died, the

145

firm's books would be given a full-scale audit, and Tuttle's crimes would be revealed. The only way he could think of to prevent that was to buy out the major's share of the partnership. If the whole firm belonged to him, he'd be safe. To be doubly safe he ruined the computer files with the water.

"When the major didn't want to sell," Frank continued, "Morris came up with a plan to convince him and you, Susan, by sabotaging the show."

"That's horrible," Susan said. "And Kenny and Boomer were working for him? I thought they were Ricky's friends."

"So did Ricky," Joe said with a grim laugh. "He didn't realize that creeps like them are for sale to the highest bidder . . . and Morris outbid him. It was Boomer and Kenny who did most of the dirty work, from sabotaging rides to putting salt in the cotton candy, and they'll spend a good long while in jail for it. Boomer's clown outfit was a perfect disguise. If they'd ever gotten caught, they could have thrown the blame on Ricky. Ricky's own dishonesty would have made it impossible for him to defend himself successfully."

"And they were responsible for the attacks on you guys?" Susan asked.

"That's right," Frank replied. "It was Boomer who set that booby trap at our house and who fired the Roman candle at me and rolled those kegs toward me. And Kenny sneaked into the Fun House car and tried to strangle me."

"And Kenny, in disguise, tried to cream me with

146

his bumper car," Joe added dryly. "He's also confessed to tampering with the safety bar on the Ferris wheel—that was a dangerous stunt."

"But it was Morris who was pulling the strings," Frank continued. "Ricky was just the fall guy."

"I had a talk with Ricky this morning," Susan said somberly. "He's going to give back all the money he took from the concessionaires and leave the show. In return, I promised not to tell Dad about what he's been doing—unless Ricky tries anything else. It's funny—he cares a lot about what Dad thinks of him. That's one reason he wanted so badly to be put in charge of the show. Maybe someday he'll learn that you have to earn respect, not get it by conning people."

Chet cleared his throat. "What about Raoul? And that guy Farkas? Did they have anything to do with Morris's scheme?"

Frank shook his head no. "Raoul is jealous of anybody who comes around Althea, that's all. And Farkas is certainly a crook, but I don't think he even knew about what Morris was doing. If he had, he would probably have tried his hand at blackmail!"

"Farkas is leaving the show, too," Susan said. "Today. We can't afford a gaffed game, even for a few more days. And I'm going to have a fair-wide meeting tomorrow and make it clear that any crooked game gets closed down on the spot. We've got a reputation to uphold."

"What about the fire?" Chet prodded. "Who pulled that off?"

147

"After knocking me out and hiding me in the House of Mirrors," Joe explained, "Boomer, in his clown getup, lured Ricky in there, knocked him out, and set the place on fire. The idea was that Ricky would be blamed for my death, the fire, and all the rest. He wouldn't be on hand to deny it. Morris would then buy the show at a bargain price. It was a pretty clever scheme."

"It would probably have worked, too," Susan said. "The only thing they didn't take into account was the wonderful detective work of Joe and Frank Hardy."

As the capsule gave a twist and swirl, Chet grinned and said, "There's something else those creeps didn't take into account. My amazing arm, and a beautiful slice of pepperoni and mushroom pizza!"